The Butterfly Hunter

The Butterfly Hunter

Janwillem van de Wetering

Houghton Mifflin Company Boston 1982

Library of Congress Cataloging in Publication Data

Van de Wetering, Janwillem,—date
   The butterfly hunter.

   I. Title.
PS3572.A4292B8   813'.54   82–7184
ISBN 0–395–32527–7   AACR2

Printed in the United States of America

S   10   9   8   7   6   5   4   3   2   1

For Juanita

PROLOGUE

The Netherlands, Summer 1933

Eddy Sachs, after absorbing a book describing imperial-
istic British battles — a present for his thirteenth birthday —
manned his soapbox racer in the garden behind the house, imitating the sound of a heavy engine and turning the wheel wildly.

A cooking pot askew on his head transformed him into a
soldier, while the racer became an armored truck spearheading
a victorious British allied column speeding through the desert.
The fleeing enemy was being slaughtered by a machine gun
fabricated from a broomstick and attached with wire to the hood
of the racer. Behind Eddy's armored car were other soldiers, invisible helpers, the comrades accompanying him during his raids.

Somebody screamed in the garage.

Eddy smiled. His hectic adventures could do with some good
screaming; a battlefield is always noisy. But only the enemy, Eddy
thought, screams. Heroes die, if at all, quietly. The cries would
be coming from Arabs, tumbling from their camels. He saw them
sprawling on the sand and triggered a last burst from his deadly
weapon. The Arabs trembled and were still. Eddy shrugged.
That's the way it goes.

"Help, Eddy!"

Eddy tore free from the threads of his imagination and jumped
from the cart. Why was his sister screaming?

"Thera?" he shouted.

3

She screamed again.

"I'm coming." He ran to the garage but the door wouldn't open. He rattled the knob. It wasn't locked; someone held it shut from the inside.

"Thera?"

The screaming stopped. Eddy ran around the garage, broke a window with a pole he found among the weeds, and forced his way into the building, pot-protected head first. He had pulled the sleeves of his jacket over his hands, to keep them from being cut on the glass.

"You don't belong here," shouted Albert, who lived next door. The pot tumbled off Eddy's head as he fought his way out of Albert's restricting embrace and climbed the stairs. Albert tried to get hold of Eddy again. "Go away, your brother says you aren't one of us."

"Let go." Eddy punched Albert; Albert staggered back. At the head of the stairs Floris waited, assuming a boxer's stance.

"Go away, Eddy."

"Why is Thera screaming?"

"You can't come up here."

Floris, Eddy's fifteen-year-old half-brother, was a dangerous antagonist and in a good defensive position. He kicked as Eddy dodged aside.

"Eddy!" The scream, cut off by a slap, gave Eddy the energy to reach the loft. He grabbed Floris's kicking leg.

"Give me a hand," Floris shouted. Other boys tore Eddy loose and dragged him across the floor.

"Tie him up."

Eddy's arms were pulled around a post and lashed with clumsy knots.

"His ankles too."

Floris pressed his fist against Eddy's nose. "Asshole! What did you come here for? You don't belong to my gang."

Floris stepped aside. Eddy saw Thera sprawled on her back on the workbench. She was naked. Her clothes lay in a crumpled heap on the sawdust-covered floor. Boys from the neighborhood stood around, grinning guiltily.

Albert stumbled up the stairs. "Sorry Floris, I couldn't hold him."

"Some guard you are, but we stopped him all the same. He can have a part too. Thera is the princess of the Shadow Lands and Eddy is the prince."

"I thought we were playing doctor," Albert said.

"Same thing," said Floris. He turned back to Eddy. "Princess Thera needs an operation. She is somewhat plugged and we have to force a way through. I have the ideal instrument." He held up an oversized carrot. Eddy pulled against his ropes. "Assistant," said Floris, "pull our patient's legs wider apart, I can't get in this way."

"Certainly, doctor."

"Assistant number two, take care that the anesthetic is properly administered."

The boy held up a dirty handkerchief. "Will this do, doctor?"

"The very thing, put it into her mouth."

Eddy heard Thera groan and saw her feet tremble convulsively. "Stop it, Floris!"

"Shut up, Eddy."

*

Eddy and Floris attended the same high school, though Floris was in a higher grade. Thera, a year younger than Eddy, went to a school for girls in another part of the city. Between Floris on one side and Eddy and Thera on the other, a one-way, easily explainable tension existed. Unlike Eddy and Thera, Floris had no real mother.

"Your mother," said Floris's father, "left a long time ago." The how and why of this situation was never discussed, although Eddy happened to overhear during a family discussion that Floris's mother was Indonesian and had mysteriously returned to her native island, exotic Borneo. A second mother appeared, a

5

witless but caring German who gave birth to Eddy and Thera. This nondescript newcomer excited Floris's fury, which he directed at his half-brother and half-sister. His angry remonstrations had no effect because Eddy and Thera ignored Floris, out of indifference rather than self-defense. The status quo persisted until the summer afternoon that framed the scene in the garage loft. After this confrontation Floris sensed a growing danger in Eddy's presence and no longer tried to annoy him. Within the Sachs home the lithe dark-complexioned boy fashioned himself into an example of diligent and moral behavior; outside he continued to be a conceited and daring character. Because he wanted to be both accepted and admired by his fellow students and was eager to avoid the staid and strained atmosphere at home, Floris stayed outdoors as much as possible and only returned for meals, or to do his homework in a room decorated with boxes that held the dry corpses of butterflies. Collecting butterflies was another motivation to be outside, because he wanted to catch the insects himself. Eddy, secretly attracted to his elegant and foreign brother, would sometimes observe him as Floris dashed through the fields or maneuvered his net while creeping between bushes.

Whenever Eddy watched Floris, he remembered the promise that he had made to himself in the garage loft. Eddy noted that Floris would dare anything and liked to gamble on the successful outcome of his heroics. But rather than the money that his exploits earned him, Floris craved continuous applause.

*

"The greengrocer's horse must have shit here a minute ago," said a boy. "Look at that, the turds are still steaming."

"Like meat croquettes," said another boy.

"Oh? Would you like a tasty croquette?" asked the first boy.

Eddy joined the group. It was recess time. The boys grinned halfheartedly, revolted by the image they had called up.

"My brother Floris will do anything," said Eddy. "He'll even eat a horse turd."

"Never."

6

"No? There he is. Ask him."

Word passed quickly and a crowd collected. Some hundred schoolboys pushed each other around the steaming heap. Floris stretched out his hand. "Ten cents a person. If I cop out I'll repay you all double."

His hand was filled with silver.

"Has everybody paid?"

Eddy surrendered a coin too. Floris didn't recognize his brother in the moving crowd.

"Just a minute," shouted the boy who had discovered the horse droppings, "I'll make the selection." He picked up a turd the size of a fist. "Here you are, Floris, enjoy your meal."

The schoolboys cheered while Floris stuffed his mouth. He chewed with determination, trying to swallow the sticky mess as fast as possible. The schoolboys staggered back, mostly silent. They were even quieter when trickles of green juice oozed from the corners of Floris's mouth. Some boys, covering their mouths, returned to the school building. Eddy stayed until the last morsel choked Floris's throat.

I made Floris eat shit, thought Eddy victoriously.

Floris's reputation increased, however. The schoolboys whispered his name with awe. The memory of his gagging face was illuminated by a shiny halo.

*

That same year Eddy's father died quite suddenly of lung cancer, and Mrs. Sachs, suffering from acute depression, was admitted into an institution. Thera became a student nurse and moved into a hospital's dormitory. Floris and Eddy, benefitting from their father's ample insurance, transferred to a private school for young gentlemen. The institute was housed in a castle, with a view of the great inland sea.

Floris, preparing for his final exams and occupying a room on another floor in the castle, seemed to have forgotten his brother's existence, and Eddy made no contact either. They didn't even see each other during the holidays. A year passed.

7

Floris swept through his exams with top grades. Traditionally the evening after the results were published was designated for a party. The castle was decorated with colored lights and flags, and the graduating class was allowed to drink alcohol. The party came to an end; the guests said good-bye; the teachers went to bed. The inebriated students collected on the castle's roof. Eddy hadn't been drinking but carefully imitated the lopsided behavior of his peers.

He leaned woozily against the crenelated wall. "Care to join me in a game of jumping the gaps?" he asked a boy who came staggering along.

"What?"

"Don't you know that game? When knights lived in this castle, it was played all the time. You climb the wall and jump the gaps, first one all around the castle wins."

The boy stuck his head out over the stone parapets. He lurched back in fright. "Jesus Christ, we're a hundred and fifty feet up here. Are you out of your mind? Nobody dares to do that."

"Floris will do it," said Eddy softly.

The members of the departing class collected in a boisterous group, holding on to each other or the wall.

"Floris, master of the castle, will address the lowly crowd," Eddy announced.

"Count Floris, our lord, we bow down to you," said one boy mockingly.

"What do I have to do?" asked Floris.

The young man who had been addressed by Eddy gestured invitingly. "Merely jump the gaps, sir. Step up here and hop all the way around. Would you dare to do that, sir?"

"I'd dare to do anything, but it'll cost you each a guilder."

The boy gathered the coins. Eddy faded back into the shadow of a niche.

Floris, filled with gin, pushed himself awkwardly onto the parapet. He stood, a silhouette swaying against the light of the rising moon and the rippled luminous surface of the great lake stretching to the horizon. He bowed to his frozen friends. "Admire me respectfully, you lowly bums."

Floris jumped. The group counted, "One. Two. Three."

What should have been "four" became, several stretched seconds later, a splash far below.

Eddy crept out of the niche and rushed down the circular stairs. Reaching the ground floor he ran into a corridor, found a classroom, and opened a window. The moat, as he had ascertained that afternoon, was filled with junk: old bicycles, discarded building materials, any useless object that had been thrown into the water by gardeners, laborers, and schoolboys. During daylight Eddy's probing hockey stick had touched solid objects everywhere in his inspection of the moat. Now, looking out into the dark, Eddy was still worried. It could be — anything is possible and the horse shit business hadn't succeeded either — that Floris at that moment would be swimming triumphantly to the drawbridge.

Floris's corpse, pierced by rusty bicycle parts, was found a little later by teachers splashing about in the shallow water.

PART 1

Amsterdam, September 1946

Clear weather, not too cool, a brilliant sun in an empty sky holding the old city like a gigantic glass cover enveloping a mature cheese — Eddy observed all this smugly; such cosmic benevolence suited his mood. If the environment had been chilly and moist, as was normal in autumn, he would have sought out the sun in Spain or, perhaps, North Africa. But as it was, the effort was unnecessary. Instead, he stretched his legs and looked about sleepily. This was the sort of weather a returning knight likes to find, the young nobleman, who, after he ties his steed to a post, enjoys himself on a flagstone balcony, protected by the spires of his castle and a wide moat. His steed was parked a little way off, a white BMW, but not too white because remains of spotty German camouflage colors were still visible on the mud-guards. The car looked magnificent, however, under the age-old plane trees growing out of the cobblestones of Leyden Square.

Here he was, the Hero, on the exclusive Tivoli terrace, resting his tired eyes on the surface of the Warden's Canal.

Eddy sighed pleasurably and looked around again. A single small cloud passing in front of the sun suddenly altered the light to a diffuse yellow glow, reminding Eddy of the patina on a Rembrandt painting. He had driven past Rembrandt's house just now, noting that the red-shuttered mansion, dating back to the

Golden Age, was badly in need of a touch of paint and partly overgrown with dying vines — a neglected dwelling, like so many of the city's prized buildings. All of Holland, he reflected, needed to be repaired. The country hadn't had time to spruce up since the German armies left, but at least it was still standing up and free again.

Germany isn't standing, Eddy thought. Germany's a plain shrouded in smoke. I'm glad I could leave.

The cloud drifted on so that the café's terrace with its cane furniture placed along harmonious lines was again bathed in crystal sunlight. Eddy felt the calming warmth of the inner town behind him, while ahead the Warden's Canal glistened, mirroring trees and elegant, gabled houses. A pity he had a headache. What had happened to the waiter? He had watched the man shuffle away quite a while back; the service in Germany was decidedly better.

Eddy tried to ignore the throbbing pain in his temples and gazed at the BMW. The previous owner of the car had more to worry about than a headache. Instead of basking in the sun on the Tivoli terrace, he would be lying on a hard bunk, between concrete walls splashed with human fluids, in the Röherstrasse jail in Hamburg, a Gestapo criminal, waiting for the noose. A miserable little runt now, but once a Germanic god. Eddy smiled in spite of his hangover. How strange that captured Nazis looked just like all other prisoners, that vanquished supermen changed so readily into weaklings.

Would the philosophers of fascism have ever considered that possibility, apart from what they experienced in dreams? Or didn't supermen dream? But of course they dreamed. The BMW was once part of their imagination, but now it was parked here, complete with legal documents that indicated he, Eddy Sachs, was the unquestioned owner. What can't be achieved with a bottle of French cognac and a little pull in the right place? Rubber stamp here, signature there, at your service, Herr Lieutenant.

"Morning, sir, coffee?" The old waiter in his shiny but perfectly pressed dark suit and clean threadbare shirt showed his badly fitting teeth.

Eddy nodded. "Please." The waiter shuffled away. "Hey ho!"

"Sir?"

"I'm not quite done, I'd also like a couple of aspirins and a Tom Collins."

The waiter observed his guest over his narrow shoulder and mumbled his agreement. His hollow-cheeked, vulpine head expressed scorn. The deeply set eyes studied Eddy. A bounder, the waiter thought; they have returned, the lovely gents.

"You won't make me wait too long, will you?"

"No, sir."

The waiter continued on his way, annoyed and feeling both unfashionable and diminished. He didn't like handsome men and abhorred the perfection of Teutonic beauty that Eddy embodied. He tried to forget Eddy's image as he mumbled the order to the bartender. Steel-blue eyes, high cheekbones, strong jaws — the combination should not be allowed. Probably a tennis pro. The waiter had recently seen a movie about tennis tournaments. This client with his wide shoulders and athletic body would have beaten the cinema champion easily; returning the most difficult shots relentlessly across the net. He could also be a paratrooper — the feature movie involved paratroopers. Well, what did it matter anyway, the fellow looked good and was expensively dressed. A tip, thought the waiter, he has to give me a good tip.

The waiter returned, smiling at imaginary bank notes floating in air, and presented the order with elegant gestures.

Eddy, wincing at the painful pressure in his head, smiled gratefully. The crushed tablets flowed down his esophagus chased by ice-cold gin and lemon juice.

"Aahh."

Right, Eddy thought, that's the way to deal with afflictions. Medicine removes pain. You can get rid of anything annoying if you just look at it from the right angle and act accordingly. Almost nobody does that, hence the misery that reigns everywhere.

He looked around for a suitable example of how not to do things. It wasn't hard to spot.

In a narrow alley leading to the terrace a young man heaved at a handcart piled high with refuse. With all his effort the fool didn't seem to be able to move the overloaded cart more than a few inches at a time on its grinding wooden wheels. Now, why would anybody ever want to try to push a cart heaped with garbage through an alley? And how could anybody permit himself to look that bedraggled? That very man, if he would only attempt to think logically, could be on this terrace at this very moment sipping the drink of his choice. That he wasn't proved that he was mad, or in any case suffering from mental poverty. That man didn't want to learn.

But I do want to learn, thought Eddy, and I've learned a lot. I have learned that circumstances, provided they are correctly assessed and usefully exploited, assist man. I have learned that the world only exists to be used.

Glancing around the terrace Eddy noted three young ladies engaged in hilarious conversation at a nearby table were smiling at him in turn. The most attractive of the three was also the most enterprising and took a moment to straighten the seam of her stocking. Eddy saw the smooth thigh and slender ankles, the suggestive twist of her hip, her breasts softly outlined in an Angora wool sweater.

He didn't return her smile. He wasn't in the right mood. It was still too early in the day. He preferred to look at the water again. Here I am, thought Eddy, and I have nothing to do. Tomorrow I'll be free as well. I can make my holiday last for weeks if I want to, but one day I'll have to get busy again. What will I be busy with? He could still think clearly, in spite of the hangover, or maybe because of it. What would he do with the days ahead? The future emerges from the past. Whoever can analyze the past with precision will know his future, isn't that right? Eddy nodded, that was correct, he would meditate on his past.

*

A few days in May 1940 had changed him from a student at the theater school into a soldier. Rifle in hand, Eddy stood ready to defend the frontiers of his country, but the thoughtless German armored columns had plowed through Holland's border somewhere else. Eddy was in the wrong place. Five days later an officer bicycling past Eddy's post informed him that it was all over and that he should surrender to the first available German soldier. The officer leaned his bicycle against a barracks wall and went inside. Eddy promptly hopped on the bicycle and was home the same day where he changed his clothes and took the girl next door for a walk.

Everything continued as he wished until a year later. He was told to work for the postmaster general in Germany. The form had been filled in clumsily and probably was a mistake, but Eddy changed his address and began dabbling in the black market and made a fair amount of money. Money still had some value; it would buy liquor and cigarettes and a bicycle. But the bicycle was stolen.

"More coffee, sir?" The old waiter had materialized again.

"Please." Eddy shook the disturbance away.

What happened afterward? An assortment of trouble — manhunts in the street and increasing pressure to work in Germany. He was arrested by bowlegged old men dressed in old-fashioned uniforms. They took him to an army barracks but didn't pay too much attention. He escaped easily. That was the time that he seriously considered leaving the local squalor and joining the Waffen SS. The SS was no good of course. But then nothing was. He had been convinced of that truth for some time. At least, the SS allowed one to perform acts of valor on the Russian tundra or in the Sahara. Germany was winning on all fronts. As a pure Aryan, blue-eyed, blond-haired, and over six feet, he would cut a dashing figure in the dark uniform. In fact, his looks protected him throughout the war.

Eddy yawned contentedly. Good is that which gives pleasure and evil the opposite — that was what he had believed in the war years and he hadn't changed his view. The incident with the boy and the uniformed Dutch Nazis had certainly had an influence. Eddy could still recall that event in detail.

*

One morning, about a year after the occupation, he saw a marching patrol of singing men in black uniforms. They were soon to be transferred to the SS and the Eastern front, and the iron-studded soles of their jackboots sounded on the cobblestone pavement with proud precision. The men were secure, fighting on what they imagined to be the right side, supported by the vast might of the fascist empire. A curly-headed patriot, maybe twelve years old, on his way to school, thought differently. He stopped to observe the patrol, stuck out his tongue, held his hands behind his ears, and yelled derisively, "Beh, beh!" The strict lines of the patrol wavered. Encouraged by these traitors' reaction the boy taunted them again. "Beat him," snapped the officer in command.

Eddy was standing next to the boy. He was shouldered away by the Nazis who flung the boy to the ground, unhooked their belts, and made them swish down on the body of their small antagonist. They continued the punishment mechanically as their stern officer watched quietly. When the lieutenant finally barked at his men, the boy lay inert on the ground, bleeding, his skull broken in various places, dead.

*

Eddy patted his pockets. He had wanted a smoke then, and the memory made him want one now. The waiter approached; Eddy pointed at the BMW. "Left my cigarettes in my car, I'll be right back."

"Certainly, sir."

Eddy sauntered off. There were no cigarettes in the car either. On his way back the attractive girl moved her arm; he rubbed against it. "Sorry."

She smiled, her tongue darting between moist lips. "That's quite all right."

Although he registered her invitation, his mind was still with the dead boy. He had wanted to defend him, but it would have been madness to interfere. What could he have done against several dozen powerful, well-armed, berserk fascist goons? What else could he have done but ignore the incident and quickly leave the scene. The demonstration of purposeless violence both turned him away from fascism and made him think of escaping.

But how did one get to England? Some friends of his planned to go by boat. They asked Eddy to join their expedition. He didn't like their sloop; it was too heavy and the engine coughed.

The friends departed. A German torpedo boat caught the sloop off the coast. Eddy heard later that his friends were shot on the beach and buried in the dunes.

On the terrace the girl was smiling at Eddy seductively. His eyes twinkled in response, while his hand gestured invitingly at the empty chair next to him. She nodded before turning back to her friends. So she would join him a little later, would she? Very well, her embrace would smooth out the pain in his head. He would take her across the square to his hotel in due course; he could still enjoy a few minutes by himself. "Waiter?"

"Sir?"

"Do you have any cigarettes?"

"They're rationed, sir. I'm afraid we're not allowed to sell them here."

Eddy produced a ten-guilder note. "I would prefer an English brand, Players or Senior Service, whatever you have."

The waiter's false teeth clacked. "One moment, sir, perhaps the doorman . . ."

*

Eddy's hunch about the heavy sloop with its faulty engine had saved his life, but he was still in Holland, still hampered by the heavy German hand tightening around the country. Air is a lighter and more promising element than water for it offers an extra dimension. Perhaps an airplane? Why not? Within a month from the execution of his friends Eddy learned during a chance

19

conversation that a certain farmer kept a plane in his barn.

He paid a call on the farmer and confirmed that the required airplane existed, apparently in excellent condition. The plane had been forced to land in his field when it ran out of fuel during the invasion and had been abandoned by its crew. The farmer hauled it out of the field with his horse and hid it in his barn. It was a Dutch plane. "The machine gun is still in it and the German know nothing." The farmer laughed slyly. "A useful tool, eh?"

"Will you give it to me?"

"What do you want to do with it?"

"Fly it to England."

"Then what?"

"I'm with the underground forces," Eddy said. "We're short of weapons and I'll fetch a good supply and come back to kill Germans."

"It's all yours," said the farmer.

Eddy's father used to say that one problem was always followed by another. But he was a somber man, a manic-depressive who might have ended as a suicide if cancer hadn't cut his life short. Eddy had taught himself to think differently. His desires programmed him positively and led him to believe that problems can always be solved, that one solution leads to the next.

Although Eddy couldn't fly, he quickly found a pilot, formerly of Royal Dutch Airlines. Eddy put his plan to the pilot at the right moment since the man had just received a letter from the commanding officer of the local German garrison. The letter invited the pilot to visit the undersigned within the next two days.

"Once they have your name," Eddy said, "you've had it. They're in need of slaves for their factories and to dig trenches on the battlefields. They won't let you fly, of course. They won't take the risk you might escape. You look like an outdoor type, I'm sure you will be equipped with a spade."

The pilot bit his nails. "You're sure it's as bad as that?"

"Worse," Eddy said, "they're after me too but I keep changing my address. Still I'm half German and could probably wrangle some easier job, but you'll be chained to a fifty-pound ball, digging ditches with a swastika embroidered on your sleeve. You're caught both ways. If the Germans lose you'll be put against the wall as a traitor."

"I can always refuse, can't I?" the pilot asked nervously.

"You can but you won't," Eddy said with a shrug, "because you value your life. We're dealing with the devil, and devils don't bargain."

"So . . . what then?"

Eddy held up a finger. "Possibility one. You'll be put to work in the open and die, for the allied planes are active and slaves can't seek shelter, they must keep working."

"Not me."

"You too. But all right. Let's assume possibility two. You refuse. The Green Police will find you, or the Feldgendarmerie. You'll be dumped in the back of a truck at three o'clock in the morning, thrown in a cell, beaten up, starved for a week, and be digging ditches after all."

The pilot nodded slowly.

"Possibility two gives you nothing," Eddy said triumphantly. "So you and I will logically select possibility three and escape to England together."

The pilot shook his head. "There's leagues of water between England and Holland and they're catching all the boats."

"My dear friend," Eddy said, grinning, "you're a pilot, you're free of the water, and I have an airplane."

"And my wife?" the pilot asked. "My children? The bastards'll take them to a camp and kill them."

Eddy swept the objection aside. "They'll travel with us. My plane has four seats. You only have two kids, haven't you? One can sit on the other's lap. We don't need luggage. England will give us liberty and everything else we need."

The pilot wanted to know what the airplane looked like. Eddy described it as accurately as he could.

"But that's insane. You're talking about a little Fokker, a reconnaissance plane. It's a worthless antique. The Jerrys have Messerschmidts and Heinkels in the sky that'll rip that poor little fly apart in two seconds."

"Not if they never see it. Not during a foggy night. It'll be foggy for the next twenty-four hours. We'll have the sky to ourselves. We'll leave tomorrow night."

"Your plane crash-landed, didn't it? How am I to get it off the ground again. There won't be enough space."

"If that plane could land on the field, it can take off from the field."

"What about gas? There hasn't been any for sale for a long time."

"Quit imagining stupid problems. All you have to do is fly, I'll take care of everything else."

The Fokker was in need of a new battery and Eddy found one. He stole a van parked behind the villa of a builder who constructed bunkers for the Germans. The builder had left his permit in the glove compartment and Eddy showed the document at various checkpoints. "You'll have to turn back," a German soldier said, "the area ahead is off limits for all civilians."

"I'm not any civilian. We're building for the Reich out there, and I need gas. Heil Hitler!" Eddy not only spoke excellent German, his commanding features and military bearing made him look more German than the soldier.

"Are you German?" the soldier asked.

"My mother is, and I'm on your side. If I weren't a good builder, I would be in uniform."

The sentry was lonely and the two men drank coffee and schnapps in the shack next to the roadblock. Afterward, Eddy filled his tank and several spare containers that happened to be in the rear of the van. I wasn't afraid, Eddy thought when he drove away, I have never been afraid. Fear is unnecessary, so much is unnecessary. It's all a piece of cake provided you know you want cake.

*

The waiter had been clearing his throat as he attempted to penetrate the veil of Eddy's thoughts. When Eddy finally noticed him the old man bowed. "The doorman only has Raleigh, sir, would that be all right?"

Eddy parted with his ten-guilder note. "Thank you, waiter."

The chairs at the next table were empty; the girls had left but he saw the beautiful one return, swaying seductively. She sat down next to him. Eddy introduced himself and appraised her while the waiter took her order. Her face was nicely chiseled but her hips seemed a trifle wide. An Old Dutch girl. Rembrandt used to paint that type of woman.

The girl engaged him in flirtatious banter. Eddy gave the right replies, flattering her outrageously, waiting for the kill. She finished her ice cream and he pointed to the Hotel Americain. "That's where I live. The rooms there are quite comfortable."

"I've never seen the rooms," the girl said, "but they're supposed to be ever so nice."

"Let me show you mine, it's a suite, the best they have."

If what she can come up with doesn't cure my headache, Eddy thought while he paid, I'll send her away and take a nap.

The sensuous way in which she uncrossed her legs and made her body rise from the chair reminded him of the old master depicting female loveliness.

The girl was smoothly passionate and responded enthusiastically to his various suggestions. "You're a very good lover," she said when she finally drew away.

"Maybe you haven't been used to much lately." Eddy grinned and reached for a cigarette on the night table. "The war has spoiled most pleasures for most people."

"Oh, not so much for me, but good lovers are rare. You know what a girl wants. You remind me of someone, but you're better than he was, and he's dead now anyway."

"A German officer no doubt." He made the statement flatly; what did he care who the girl had slept with?

"How did you guess?" The girl sat up and stared at him.

"You said he was dead, didn't you? More Germans died than Dutch. I believe the figure is ten million against several thousand, not counting Jews."

"Hans," the girl said. "He was very sweet, but they sent him to Russia and he only wrote to me once. Later I heard that his division was completely destroyed, near Stalingrad somewhere. Everybody died out there, didn't they?"

Eddy caressed a nipple. "Hitler's orders, no surrender. I remind you of him, do I?"

She sighed. "You're better looking, but he was more gentle.

Still, you are similar in a way; that's why I kept on smiling at you on the terrace, I couldn't help myself."

The nipple failed to stiffen. "Are you tired?"

"A little. You won't mind if I doze off for a while, do you?"

"Be my guest." He turned away and watched the ceiling where the sunlight reflected by the canal produced a network of interesting lines. The girl had said that she wanted to go dancing later in the evening, but he planned to get rid of her. Rather than hopping about in some shoddy establishment he would prefer to stay in his room and ponder his future. A glow spread through his body and made his skin tingle. Groaning with satisfaction he stretched himself under the sheet and his thoughts returned to his memories.

*

He was back in the small plane taking off faultlessly, even though the farmer's field offered little space and trees half hidden by ground fog posed dangerous obstacles. Once the Fokker was free of the ground the flight became uneventful. The pilot's wife kept the kids quiet so that Eddy, his tension lulled by the drone of the plane's engine, nodded off, until the pilot nudged him awake.

"When the British see us they'll shoot us down. Maybe I should keep as low as I possibly can."

"Don't worry," said Eddy yawning, "all the risks are behind us, just keep going."

The clouds were heavy over the British coast, and the Fokker flew on unnoticed until it touched down on a military airfield near Canterbury, Kent, after nearly colliding with a Spitfire taking off on a routine patrol. Eddy waved at soldiers who came running toward them, shouting and brandishing their Sten guns. "It's all right, we are Dutch! From Holland."

It proved to be a drunken night. The farmer had poured genever before saying good-bye, and the squadron leader officially welcomed them with whiskey. Later on there was yet more to drink, offered by security officers who then, reluctantly and politely, arrested the new arrivals.

"You really don't mind, do you?" they asked. "It's merely a matter of routine."

"Go right ahead," Eddy said, draining his glass.

The pilot and his family disappeared in a separate car, and Eddy was driven to a London cell, which he left the next day. Acquaintances living in England guaranteed his good intentions. He was directed to the Dutch Club and met an officer of the Netherlands Military Police who in turn introduced him to a general in charge of overseas operations. The general suffered from a chronic cold and sneezed continuously. His watery eyes stared at Eddy, their lack of expression repeated by the glassy gaze of sculptured lions supporting his desk. The imbecilic smile of a poor portrait of the queen of the Netherlands dominated the dingy office.

"Your health, general."

"Thank you. Do you have German blood?"

"My mother is German."

The general studied his moist handkerchief. "Happens in the best of families, Sachs, but you're cleared so you must be okay. Would you like to be a spy?"

The general sneezed several times while Eddy formulated his refusal. The general didn't appear to hear what Eddy said. "Fine, fine. The way you look the job should be easy. You'll find my adjutant in the office next door, he will arrange matters." Eddy shook his head and began to speak. "Never mind," the general said kindly, "please go now, you don't want to catch my cold."

During the next three months Eddy forgot his lack of enthusiasm while drinking lukewarm pints of bitter in the house bar of a villa on the Cornish coast, in between playing games. The purpose of each game was to kill your opponent quickly. The teachers were good-tempered, quiet guerrillas — noncommissioned commando officers on indefinite leave from the North African front because of physical handicaps caused by battle wounds. They soon pronounced Eddy the establishment's undisputed champion, not only because their new recruit tore apart every stuffed dummy masquerading as a German soldier no matter how placed or where hidden, but also because Eddy added to their bag of tricks. The "Dutch demigod," as he was called in the encampment, invented a grip which, by using the angled neck protector of the German helmet as a lever, efficiently snapped the enemy's neck. Eddy won a prize for this innovation, a free date with the barmaid. Eddy appreciated the gesture because the girl, pretty and free of competition, was used to overcharging for her services. When he proved himself to be a crack shot and also managed to ride a motorcycle down the face of a cliff without either wrecking the machine or himself, the guerrillas returned him to London with special recommendation.

The general hadn't moved from his desk; his cold had worsened and he had lost his voice. He scribbled a note which Eddy delivered to the adjutant.

Eddy floated down, a parachute-held particle in the northeastern Dutch sky; around him others descended gracefully toward their home soil. Down below the Sicherheitsdienst, tipped off by a London-based traitor, waited impatiently.

A vagrant breeze pushed Eddy's parachute away from the main body and caused him to land behind a cluster of birch trees, out of sight of the German military. The Cornish guerrillas had taught him much but failed to instill a sense of direction, so he strayed even further and thereby escaped the welcoming but ultimately fatal arms of the enemy.

Eddy discovered a luxurious mansion whose lights peeped through the tears in the paper that blacked out its windows. Peering through one of the rents he saw a well-built, middle-aged gentleman. The gentleman sat in front of an open fire, reading a newspaper, and appeared to be alone.

Eddy rang the doorbell. The gentleman opened the door while knocking ash from his dark red velvet waistcoat. "Yes? Still about at this time of night? It's after curfew you know, you're lucky you didn't run into a patrol."

"I got lost," Eddy said.

"Come in, dear fellow."

"A drink?" the benevolent host asked when his guest had joined him in front of the fireplace.

"Please. You have a lovely house."

"I should have, I'm the mayor of our town and head of the local Nazi party. I trust you share our modern ideas."

"Not officially," Eddy said. "I don't believe in joining any group, but I do sympathize with some of the new creed."

Eddy was asked to stay. The food came out of imported tins, and the mayor poured a good wine. As it was the weekend, his host was free from work. He was a voluble man and seemed to be satisfied with Eddy's statement that he was on holiday, staying with acquaintances in a nearby city, and had lost his way during a hike in the country. The mayor changed the subject to literature, explaining that he was a fan of the mystery and spy genres. It was late when the mayor took Eddy to his room.

Eddy heard the mayor talking on the telephone the next morning. The mayor spoke in German. "Right, I'm glad you let me know, Herr Hauptmann. See you tomorrow." After the evening meal, which included much wine, the mayor poured cognac and warmed his bottom at the fire. "Tell me, do you carry a weapon?"

Eddy had left his Browning pistol under the mattress in the guest room. "No."

"I do. Would you like to see it?"

Eddy realized too late that he should have refused. The mayor was showing him his erection.

"Aha," said Eddy.

"Don't you think this is a proud and splendid spectacle?"

Eddy had no ready answer.

"And appetizing?"

"Perhaps, but I'm not from that side of the fence."

The mayor executed several small dance steps. "Anybody can learn anything, you don't know what you're missing."

Eddy smiled noncommittally. The mayor unbuttoned his fly even farther. "This isn't just a weak joke, you know. I really do

28

carry a weapon here. Look." He maneuvered his hand under his genitals and produced a small revolver.

"Well I'll be damned," Eddy said; "what a strange place to carry a gun."

"On the contrary. Now this is something I learned from a spy writer who knew his trade. The holster has been specially made for me by a craftsman in the village. It's attached to my thigh, you see, and held by another strap around my hips." The mayor danced closer. Eddy made an effort not to move away.

"Don't be shy," the mayor said. "I'm demonstrating useful knowledge. My gun is small but it's deadly enough. Aren't you a spy yourself? Well now, if they ever catch you they won't go for your balls immediately, not even when they adhere to Greek principles, and even then they'll wait till later. Consequently, you'll have an opportunity to surprise your enemy."

The mayor pirouetted and retreated a little.

"Am I a spy?" asked Eddy.

"But of course you are. The German garrison commander told me that spies had been dropped in the area and that all of them except one are accounted for. You are the exception, but you're safe with me. I'm not quite as fanatical as my colleagues."

The mayor's erection pointed at Eddy once more; his revolver didn't. Eddy made his lips curl lasciviously and his eyes shine invitingly. "Let's not be hasty, we hardly know each other."

The mayor scowled. "Don't tease. You simply have to give in right now. Nothing for nothing, right? Surely you have accepted that principle of fascism. Facts are facts. I'm an official Nazi risking my career by wining, dining, and hiding you here."

Eddy tempered his smile. "I'm in complete agreement, but don't you think pleasure increases when it's a bit prolonged? Why be so hasty? We have all night."

The mayor holstered his gun and replaced his penis. He turned away to button his fly. "Very well, we'll play it your way. Let me get a bottle that I inherited from a titled relative, it has been waiting for company such as yours. You're quite attractive, you know, and probably intelligent as well. Our shared experience should take us to dizzy heights."

"Good idea," Eddy said while watching amber liquid pouring from an unlabeled dusty bottle.

The mayor raised his glass solemnly but became talkative again. He expounded the philosophy of power, singing the praise of amoral simplicity. He paused, looking for even better and more subtle words.

Eddy interrupted the intellectual flow. "And you joined the Nazi party because of all that?"

The mayor hesitated. "Perhaps not."

"So what was the real reason?"

The mayor had to think for a moment. "Because I'm a sadist."

Eddy gestured drunkenly and excusingly. "Your affliction can't be too bad, you appear to be kindness personified."

The mayor closed one eye and held a finger next to his nose. "Oh, but I am a secret sadist."

Eddy grinned and slouched in his chair. "So what do you do?"

The mayor refilled their glasses and rubbed his hands. "Before I go to bed, I beat up a chair with my belt."

"And what do you imagine when you do that? Boys?"

The mayor raised a protesting hand. "Never. The very thought, would I hurt the beautiful little fellows who I love? No, I see my mother, and sometimes . . ."

"Yes?" Eddy asked eagerly.

"My aunt."

Eddy laughed, as did the mayor. The mayor was approaching Eddy on his knees. "A terrible woman, but I'm getting even with her. I'll get even with you too in a moment, you beautiful pure-blooded Aryan, not with my belt but with my big —"

Eddy hit the mayor's head hard and his host toppled over on his side. Eddy slid down from his chair.

"You scoundrel," the mayor groaned.

Eddy hit him again with the side of his hand. "If you get him behind the ear," a Cornish commando sergeant had said, "your victim will sort of gurgle for a while, but the sound is mechanical. He is in fact dead."

The mayor gurgled.

"Don't hold it against me," Eddy said, unbuttoning the mayor's fly, "but you didn't really give me a choice, did you? I'll leave you your pride, but I will take your gun and holster."

"And your car," he said half an hour later when he was ready to leave the house, "as it will allow me to slip through the checkpoints. The money you hid in your Bible will ease my way too." He bent over the corpse. "How sweet and pleasant you look now, your mother and aunt will be happy to see you."

*

The sky sheltering Amsterdam was overcast and the lines on the white ornamental tin-stamped ceiling of the room in the Hotel Americain had faded away. Eddy's skin no longer tingled and he felt cold under the sheet. The girl next to him was snoring gently. He shook her shoulder. "You'll have to go now." She tried to embrace him but his arm blocked her approach.

"Weren't we supposed to go out together?"

"I'm sorry, I'd forgotten I had an appointment."

She sat up. "Shall we meet tomorrow again?"

"Perhaps. Leave me your telephone number."

He watched her dress, kissed her briefly, and shut the door behind her.

The room stayed cold, even after he had closed the window and turned up the radiator. He took a shower but the hot water warmed only his skin.

Eddy didn't give in to the suddenly dismal atmosphere. He put on his bathrobe and shaved leisurely. When he came back to his room rain was splattering against the windows. He lit a cigarette, phoned room service for coffee and fried eggs on toast, and dropped back onto the bed.

The dear mayor had been useful to him. If he'd only been able to go back to relate his adventure, the commando guerrillas from Cornwall would have procured the most beautiful girl from the county for their disciple.

But while the mayor was dead his advice lived on; Eddy heeded it about a month later so that another man could die. The Gestapo raided a bar where Eddy was drinking at the expense of Dutch underground army officers. The bar was a private club and only insiders were supposed to know its location, but a prisoner who'd been tortured too long had given the secret away. When the sudden entry of shouting, weapon-waving German detectives caused the resistance officers to panic and surrender, Eddy stayed seated, sipping his drink, and was almost overlooked.

"May I please take a leak before we leave?" Eddy asked the Gestapo officer who finally noticed him.

The detective granted the request, uttered softly in faultless German, and followed his prisoner into the restroom. Eddy detached the mayor's small gun, turned as if he wanted to make a casual remark, pressed its muzzle against his captor's belly, and fired. The German looked surprised as he crumpled slowly to the floor. Eddy left the toilet and jumped through a window at the rear of the building, one floor down into the street. He walked away slowly, turned the wrong corner, and passed the Germans, kicking their prisoners into a waiting truck. They were too busy to notice the tall man walking by quietly. Meanwhile their colleague died slowly, hiccupping and blowing bloody bubbles while he frantically tried to remember what had caused him to give in so foolishly to a dangerous prisoner's inadmissible request.

Eddy, puffing placidly on his cigarette, smiled at the memory. He had not been a perfect warrior, for his arrest had shaken him enough to make the wrong turn once he was out in the street, but again his lack of fear in a crisis had pushed him over the hurdles. As he had walked away from the truck, he had had time to contemplate his own magnificence. So he had made a mistake, but he corrected it immediately. There is nothing wrong with arrogance, as long as it rests on valid experience. Was that the day that the advertising agent got hold of him? No, it must have been later, somewhere else in Amsterdam.

"Sir, sir," called the man.

"Yes?"

"Would you step into my office for a moment?"

"Why?"

"You are exactly the type I've been searching for. You have the look. I need you to model for me . . . for advertising. I'll pay well."

Eddy was temporarily issued a smart StutzStaffel uniform and taken to a large yard behind a German barracks where he was told to stand under the protruding barrel of a tank's cannon. He smiled obediently and assumed the prescribed attitude, shoulders straight, legs apart. Later, back at the collaborating advertiser's office, he netted an extra fee by helping to create the poster's slogan: *You are free, thanks to me.*

While the posters displaying Eddy's Nazi image perverted the minds of these young Dutchmen who wondered whether or not to join the dreaded but famed Waffen SS, Eddy continued to spy. Knowing that he was too spectacular to move about incognito, he didn't bother to change his appearance. Instead he relied on his resemblance to the Nazi ideal to help him collect information useful to the allies. He noted the numbers of German army units, estimated available quantities of material, traced troop movements, discovered rocket launching sites, and memorized the addresses where high-ranking Nazi officers lived or amused themselves. His notes, translated into code, were telegraphed to London by a schoolteacher. The schoolteacher was betrayed by a jealous girlfriend; Eddy seduced her and was in turn betrayed because he shared the schoolteacher's habit of changing bedmates frequently. The continuing necessity to move about was a good reason to be unfaithful.

"Our batteries must be recharged continuously," he once said to the schoolteacher, "so we need to plug in to any suitable outlet we happen to find along our way, otherwise our voltage goes down and we're no longer effective."

The Sicherheitsdienst tried to arrest him while he was with the girl, but the German occupation was coming to an end and their secret service was short of manpower; only two agents were available and they charged the house without being protected by any back-up in the street. From the girl's nervous behavior Eddy understood that she had left the front door open to ease his arrest. He knocked her out and, holding his gun, hid in a cupboard in the corridor. He shot the two detectives in the back as they rushed past his hiding place, but he didn't kill the woman.

Eddy snubbed out his cigarette, got up, and paced around the hotel room. He spent a minute looking out of the window, admiring two swans floating gracefully on the canal's surface touched by shreds of the evening fog. It was still raining lightly and he was still tired. He lay down again.

Why hadn't he killed the woman? The mayor's gun only held five cartridges of an unusual caliber that Eddy couldn't obtain anywhere at the time. When he faced the woman, dressing before he left the house, he had only two cartridges left. That's why she was still alive, married now and changed into a tidy Dutch housewife intent on having dinner ready on time.

Eddy dozed and then suddenly woke again. It was dark in the room and he switched on the light on his night table. He was sweating. Dreaming of the war, he had seen a long file of Jews, trudging along in the direction of the Amsterdam railway station. Unguarded, they were obediently following instructions sent to them by mail, sheep herding themselves.

He brushed his wet hair back with his fingers, desperately trying to think reasonably, to forget that one of the hopelessly shuffling figures had been himself. "I'm not a Jew," he said aloud, "and if I were I would not have been caught that way, or any other way. When I saw those fools I knew that the system that was hauling them in to the gas chambers was foolish too. I knew the Nazis would fail, that the craziness would trip itself up." He sat up, mumbling stupidly. The grotesque dream's imagery had to be senseless. That figure that he recognized between the doomed Jews could not have been himself, for he was not connected with the tragedy, any tragedy.

He forced himself to smile. If the Germans, that stolid fanatic race, would not see that the purpose of life is pleasure, if it wasted its time and energy on unamusing perversions, such as the extermination of Jews, that was *their* mistake.

His head dropped back on the pillow — another memory flashed through his mind. He saw a German officer boarding a streetcar. An old gentleman was trying to get in too; he lost his balance and stumbled against the officer. The German saw the yellow star sewn on the man's coat, cursed, and hit the Jew in the face. The old man staggered back and fell. The clarity of the dream made Eddy squeak with fear. How could the victim's emaciated face resemble his own? How could this crushed figure sprawling in the mud mirror his being, not only in bizarre symbolism but in stark reality? But the picture, three-dimensional, finely shaded in color, left no room for doubt. The old man's wavy hair was Eddy's, so were his blue eyes, so were his flailing limbs. Eddy, the dreamer, studied the dream. Then there was no duality anymore — he had become the old man and acutely felt his pain. There was much detail in the experience; he saw his hand hit the metal side of a mailbox, next to the tramstop.

Eddy sat up again; his hand had hit the metal side of the night table.

"Enough," Eddy said quietly. He got up and dressed, banishing all further horrors by promising himself another Tom Collins in the café across the street.

Eddy crossed the square, determined to shake off the darkness of the slowly dissolving shadows of his nightmare. The city looked ominous now; night clouds brooded low over the gray shapes of buildings lining the space around him. Even the square itself had changed appearance and was cluttered by raucously clanging streetcars and automobiles growling angrily. The lights of the Tivoli terrace attracted him, and he quickened his pace to reach the comfort of its welcoming safety. The old waiter was still there, standing motionless between the cane chairs, a priest guarding a shrine. The relaxed postwar feeling of the terrace, the slow heavy traffic on the square lit by streetlights, and the rhythmical flashes of neon advertising all disappointed Eddy, and his thoughts naturally returned to the hectic activity of his recent past.

"All good things come to an end," the Dutch general said when Eddy came to say good-bye when the war was over. The general had installed himself in The Hague, but his office was just as musty as his former Whitehall quarters. He was again surrounded by stupidly staring, malformed lions, while another badly drawn image of Queen Wilhelmina contemplated Eddy sadly from a cracked plaster wall. The general also retained his cold. "But you're still useful to us, Sachs, and I think we'll hold on to you a little longer." The general coughed and mumbled.

"General?"

"Lieutenant?"

"Is that what I am now?"

"But of course," the general said kindly. "I've put stars on your shoulders and am sending you to Germany. In a way, spies are evil men. It pleases me to make you a virtuous man for a change. You'll be after war criminals. It's time for the prey to become the hunter."

The general signed a document and made a telephone call, then lapsed into solitary mumbling.

"General?"

"Kindly leave me with my bronchitis, lieutenant. My adjutant will be waiting for you outside and will do what is necessary."

Eddy rode into Hamburg, safe behind the oversized shoulders of a Dutch military police sergeant, in a large, recently confiscated Opel. The car cut through the thin mixture of smoke and dust of crumbled building material that seemed to be all that was left of Hamburg's inner city and eventually reached a suburb, overlooked in parts by allied bombers.

Eddy's destination, a sumptuous villa overlooking a small river, the Kleine Alster, was a good example of late art deco, with wide wavy lines reminiscent of an old-fashioned radio set, surrounded by a meticulously kept park situated near a pond and nestled in lush foliage. Eddy smiled at his new surroundings, so different from what he had expected Germany to be.

"This is your destination, lieutenant," the sergeant said briskly. "There is no sign on the door because this is the local headquarters of Allied Security. That's your outfit, isn't it, sir?"

"So I was told." Eddy followed the giant, trying to march in step up the marble stairs.

"They must be having a party in there," the sergeant said after he had pressed the doorbell. Eddy listened to the music reverberating in the villa. "Dance music? In the afternoon?"

The sergeant grinned. "We've won the war so we're supposed to have a good time. It's our turn now, sir."

The party continued all through the year that Eddy lived in the villa, though some work was done from time to time. Imitating the methods of his allied colleagues, Eddy waited for the

Nazis to betray themselves. Mere membership in the Nazi party now constituted a crime, and the suspects who were brought in, often by regular German police detectives, were grilled in order to extract details from their official past so that the charges against them could be expanded. As the Nazis excelled in shifting the blame among themselves and had usually failed to destroy their extensive files, Eddy's job was simple enough, and he was soon busy organizing massive arrests. Important or wealthy suspects tried to bribe their interrogators, and the security officers accepted everything. Jealousy among themselves, however, restricted their greed so that most loot was surrendered to their chief, the Polish colonel Piasecki. Piasecki controlled the stream of gold and goods and made most of it flow back to finance the villa's routine. The colonel liked women and had them supplied by the busload, to strip and dress them again with evening dresses and fur coats confiscated from the suspects.

"I'm an economist," a French captain said, "and I like doing this sort of thing. The circulation of goods is absolutely necessary to healthy housekeeping."

"Fuck 'em all," said an OSS man in mufti, "and let them yak away in the meantime, those gals like to show off. All you have to say is that you don't believe them and they'll provide you with proof. Yesterday I was given the address of some minor Führer of the Gestapo, the guy was actually there. I wouldn't call this an investigation anymore; it's more like picking apples."

"We get apples," the Frenchman said, "but the melons always seem to roll away." His arm swept around his luxurious surroundings. "Our invisible host is a melon."

"Freiherr von Wittenberg?" Eddy asked.

"*Exactement.*" The French captain stood at attention for a moment. "A simple Wehrmacht general, but a big thief, and especially interesting to you, because he stole in the Low Countries, monsieur, in your own *territoire.*"

"I know it," Eddy said, "but according to my information he is far out of reach."

"La Suisse?"

39

"Never," the OSS man said. "Sure, he was in Switzerland for a while, but he's now drinking bourbon in our embassy in Asunción, Paraguay. A good friend of the local Führer over there, who is our friend again."

The Frenchman raised his right arm. "*Heil*, President Stroesner."

"They're still with us," a British officer said, "and we'll probably facilitate their return ourselves. Every man is half a Nazi."

The international gathering's attempt at philosophizing bored Eddy and he wandered away, looking for a more pleasant subject to concentrate on. The servants of the villa were preparing a cold buffet. Eddy checked the delicacies on display. "Are there no sardines?"

An old butler looked at him worriedly and pointed at the various dishes. "Russian caviar, Norwegian mackerel, Canadian crab, Dutch smoked eel."

"But no sardines, you're not doing a good job, Uncle Franz."

The butler smiled subserviently; if Herr Lieutenant was calling him by his nickname, the powerful officer might not be as displeased as he pretended to be. He clicked his heels. Eddy checked his watch.

It was time to go to the Röherstrasse jail, an underground maze of stone corridors lined with cells that had survived the bombing. It would be an easy afternoon, to be filled mostly with formalities. Several suspects found guilty of atrocities committed against Jews, Polish civilians, or even prisoners of war were ready to be marched to the platform where nooses moved gently in the draft. Fresh cases had come in again, however. The endless wave of accusations contained in neatly typed reports prepared by articulate and disciplined German secretaries began to choke Eddy. No one who had been part of the fascist apparatus could go free, and every prisoner seemed destined, according to reestablished legal structure, to the death penalty or perpetual imprisonment. Perhaps Colonel Piasecki, who liked to drink vodka diluted with Coca-Cola when lecturing, was right when he suggested that one mass grave should be dug, large enough to hold the entire German population. Afterward the grave could be filled, raked, and planted with wheat. The grave could be even larger, Eddy thought, to make room for other troublesome tribes, the Russians for instance.

Mollified by this all-encompassing solution he stopped and studied a painting hanging in a dark corner of the hall. The portrait returned his stare. Unpleasantly fascinated, Eddy tried to identify the painting's subject. The portrait, dashingly depicted in once flamboyant colors, had lost some of its splendor due to a layer of solid dust, so most of its background was invisible. The man had to be a king because he wore a crown. Examining it more closely, Eddy was surprised to see that the king resembled himself, although the face seemed smoother and more feminine. This must be my royal, biblical, and homosexual ancestor, Eddy thought, or is the homosexual overtone only due to his long hair?

The king was older than Eddy, in his thirties probably, but the resemblance was striking — the same wide, sensuous mouth, the same blue rather slanting eyes, and the same proud intro-verted expression. Eddy grinned. This fellow would have liked a bit of pleasure too, and he was certainly not stupid. Rather an attractive type in a way. Eddy flicked his lighter and peered again — the hard jaw expressed strength, tempered by the sen-sitive eyes and soft line of the lower lip. Eddy squeezed his of-ficer's stick a little tighter under his arm and tore himself free from his observation. An earlier incarnation? Or an image from the future?

He walked on. A servant on hands and knees following a rag dipped in floor polish obstructed his way. Eddy noticed that he had to restrain himself. Another representative of the vanquished foe now politely inviting a kick in the ass. He refused to give in to the temptation, for logical reasons. If he damaged this servant, there would be nobody to clean the floor.

"Excuse me," he said in a clipped voice.

The man moved obsequiously to the side.

Eddy walked to his car, proud that he had again succeeded in avoiding senseless violence. The four scratch marks on the butt of the gun he still carried in addition to his service revolver didn't count. The four dead bodies left in Holland were the logical result of forceful causes, of logical choices that circumstances had offered. Some violence serves a purpose, most doesn't; kicking servants' asses clearly fitted the second category. Besides, he found that type of activity ultimately distasteful. Hadn't he made a rule never to do anything that he didn't enjoy? He didn't play poker, for instance, an occupation which consumed much of the security officers' leisure time in the villa at the Kleine Alster.

There were other enjoyable pursuits, however. He enjoyed cruising through the city in his gleaming BMW and admiring the women who kept themselves available at any hour of the night or day to please the foreign soldiers. At times he selected some especially attractive whore.

He also enjoyed reading his books on psychology, a collection which had once formed part of his training at the Amsterdam Theater School, which the war had interrupted. He had found the books again after the liberation and now kept them on a shelf behind his bed, taking time every now and then to study a chapter or flick through his notes. He thought of himself as an archeologist making great discoveries in vast subconscious territories. These analytical expeditions, guided by the experts in the field, aroused his powers of concentration. The suddenly visible gallery of demons from his unconscious amused him.

He had to stop at an intersection on his way to the jail and wait as a long irregular column of men dressed in rags, staring ahead listlessly with hollow eyes, emerged from a railway station — prisoners of war belatedly returned by Russia. There they go, Eddy thought, the German demons. They burned the Ukraine down and were almost destroyed in turn, but there is still much potential strength in them. They can be manipulated again.

Like my own demons, he thought a while later, edging the BMW forward, honking his horn to force a passage through the shuffling crowd of invalids. But mine are in better shape, carefully packed in cotton wool in a drawer of my soul, ready to be used properly whenever I need them.

42

The pleasant part, the cheerful element in Eddy's repeated meetings with Obersturmbahnführer Paul Kroll, was that the former officer of the Waffen SS did not seem to be overly concerned with his present predicament. He never cried when the turnkeys ignored his meal times and never crawled on the floor or threw up in fear when the guards made him the butt of their sadistic pranks. Eddy always found Kroll in the same position, solidly seated on his bunk and leaning against the wall.

"Good day," Eddy said.

"Good day, Herr Lieutenant, did you bring cigarettes?"

"Yes, right here."

"Excellent. I don't have a light either."

"Here you are."

Kroll inhaled the smoke and began to cough. "Pretty strong, this English tobacco. How are you people doing outside?"

"Bit of a drizzle," Eddy said, "and most everything is still in ruins. You're better off here."

The large, broad-shouldered officer grinned and rubbed his closely clipped skull. "Really? I'd still rather be outside. The treatment here doesn't improve at all. Why don't you let me go? If I've ever broken the Geneva Convention, it was in Russia, and you'll never get me to talk about that. The papers you have in there," he pointed to Eddy's briefcase, "don't even mention that part of my career. I'm here because I disobeyed my Führer's orders to stupidly die in the lost battle of Stalingrad and, moreover, contravened Field Marshal Paulus's instructions to surrender. I got out and stayed out, even out of the Gestapo's hands. The staff officers who never left their tea-party bunkers in the Fatherland will never forgive me for being an original, so they gave me to you. My sin was no sin at all. It was a good thing to get out of that mess, and such business is still an internal German affair. To keep me here is a mistake which you may as well admit."

"Now now," Eddy said, not bothering to hide his amusement.

Kroll answered in the same tone of voice. "Now now is right. Just let me go, you'll have another cell at your disposal, room to keep somebody you can get your teeth into."

Eddy allowed the silence to ooze back into the small cell. He knew from the first time he met Kroll that he could easily identify with the SS man, both mentally and emotionally — it seemed as if he and Kroll had developed along parallel lines and were perhaps still doing so. He faked a yawn. "Let you go, eh? And what will your liberty do for me?"

Kroll pretended to look bored too. "It will provide you with money."

"Do you have any?"

"Right now," Kroll said, "I'm flat broke. But what is money? Money is an apparition that you can materialize by relating events and holding on to the connections. As soon as I'm outside I'll be busy gathering wealth."

Eddy laughed. "You haven't been outside for a while, there isn't much going for people like you. What do you think you are, a magician?"

Kroll's square nails scratched through the stubble on his chin. "No, but I'm a Kraut, a Kraut who is at home. We are reconstructing the rubble and pretty soon I'll be happily active, pushing and pulling until I manage to set up a bar. I'll call it the Free Eagle. I can see it all now. But the first push is yours, nothing for free, of course. As soon as I'm up and about I'll be somebody again, somebody you might find useful one day."

Their sudden intimacy did not irritate Eddy; on the contrary, he appreciated their closeness, as if he valued the enemy's trust. He also recognized the possibility that his opponent was superior to himself and that it was important not to show his weakness. He blew smoke at the flies buzzing around his head. "Why should I believe you?"

Kroll's hands joined on his stomach while he smiled slowly. "Why shouldn't you believe me? We are both intelligent adventurers and no longer on different sides of the fence. The whole world is open to us and we'll both be taking risks again. I need you now. You will need me later."

"This is too vague for me," Eddy said. "Let's fix an amount and a date. You said you would pay me in money. How much did you have in mind?"

The smile on Kroll's wide mouth became more pronounced. He raised a hand in slow protest. "You're younger than I am, Herr Lieutenant, let me warn you, money is a vague term. You may not even be wanting it. My promise to you will go beyond marks or sterling, I will provide whatever help you need at whatever time you need it."

Eddy could not remember now what else had been said during the conversation. He did remember that he had released the prisoner and how Kroll, bent and fearful, prodded by guards, walked to Eddy's BMW. Ten minutes later Kroll was out on the streets of Hamburg with all the cash Eddy happened to have on him.

"Give me a year," Kroll said before he left the car, "by that time I'll be in the telephone book. Look for the Free Eagle."

They shook hands. "See you," Eddy said.

The encounter with SS officer Kroll was one of the better moments in a pleasant period, Eddy thought as he searched his memory for similar episodes. The noise of the streetcar bells on Leyden Square cut through his reverie. A beggar pumping plaintive music out of a hand organ reminded him of the villa at the Kleine Alster, where his peace had also been continuously disturbed, either by relentless partying or by the radios and gramophones of his colleagues. He recalled how at night the villa took on a cheap, garish glow from the garlands of pink lightbulbs hung in the garden, and how he had been irritated by its open fireplaces protected by aprons of thin bronze strips, its flimsy decorations painted on whitewashed walls above the ornate paneling, the bookcases filled with expensively bound and never touched works of art, purchased by the yard and sorted by color. Had the garish interior ever been more than a saccharine-sweet background for equally artificial and everlasting merrymaking?

He remembered an evening that only differed from many others in a few particulars. Groups of dress-uniformed officers formed rest points between butterfly-like ladies whose transparent clothes appeared even more erotic in the light of tall red candles. The general mood seemed jollier than usual; perhaps there was some event to celebrate; had they caught a supercriminal that day or was the elation due to a run of unusually good weather? The free

46

liquor made everybody's skin glow. Dancing was in progress. Later that night there would be a striptease contest judged by an intricate point system, with the favorites being awarded to the winner of a lottery among the officers. There were no bounds that night. The music throbbed a travesty of blues played by native jazzmen to the beat of military marches. The victors suffered from a rush of power, somewhat contained by Colonel Piasecki's presence. The colonel interrupted the program from time to time to sing sad ballads, accompanying himself on guitar. Other Poles performed a national dance, shouting and hopping about on their haunches; the French contributed to the festivities by squeezing or slapping female bottoms. A Scottish major admonished them. "Stop that, you don't hit pigs either, blue spots diminish the value of their meat."

"Zis is going too far," a Dutch captain said, imitating the well-known German accent of the princely commander of his armed forces. "Don't you think so, Sachs?"

"Not yet." Eddy brought the cognac ordered by his superior, warming the fat glass with his hands. "But the French do rather behave as if they were at home."

"And the Americans seem to think they are in the Wild West again." The captain's head pointed in the direction of a portly warrior dressed in neat army green who was demonstrating the mechanics of a Schmeisser machine pistol on the highly polished top of a sculptured oak table. "That same fellow destroyed the rear wall of the garden yesterday, using a German bazooka. The fragments of the shell hit a shanty on the other side of the water. We haven't heard anything yet, but I wouldn't be surprised if there were several wounded. Those shacks are filled with civilians. Won't do much for our reputation, you know."

Reputation, Eddy thought, what reputation? They gassed six million Jews and beat five million Poles to death. Aren't we allowed to damage a few civilians by mistake?

"Ha, ha," the captain said, "look, that *is* amusing. I'll join in, I think."

He ran to the stairs at the rear of the hall leading to the gallery that surrounded the vast room on all sides. The Polish and French officers had found two lazyboys set on casters and divided themselves in teams. Each team consisted of a rider and a pusher and the finish line was marked with palms growing out of copper pots. Again and again the improvised carts raced to their goal while the public downstairs gambled on the outcome.

"My turn, I say," the captain shouted.

Eddy grabbed the other vehicle and asked an Englishman with an RAF moustache to push him.

He won, but the Englishman turned the cart and released it so that it bounced down the stairs. Eddy's pride would not allow him to jump free. In order to increase his safety he grabbed one of the potted palms, hoping that its weight would provide some stability. It did not. The heavy palm increased his speed and made his crash more spectacular. Its exploding earth dirtied his uniform.

"Never mind, old boy." The British officer brushed him off solicitously with a bundle of ostrich feathers that he pulled out of the hair of a lady who happened to be within reach. The girl smiled pathetically at Eddy in a mute plea for help. Eddy, still dizzy from his ride, refused to restore her dignity and brushed her hand from his sleeve. He walked away. The party was about to end, but the villa's tradition demanded a last period of Extreme Liberty, which was really no more than a general display of female nakedness, celebrated in the final dance where pink flesh was pressed to the harsh texture of various uniforms.

The ladies didn't mind undressing provided their expensive clothes weren't damaged. Servants, imperturbable within their discipline, continued to fetch and carry, ignoring the melee.

The music stopped, drowned in applause. The sudden silence woke the American, almost out of view in his easy chair. He jumped up and grabbed the submachine gun that was still on the table. He selected a victim and pointed the weapon. "You come with me." The luscious blond, impressed by the Schmeisser's cruel gleaming barrel stabbing her navel, was ready to surrender, but the officer, distracted by a commotion on the dance floor, quickly forgot her and wandered away. She faced Eddy and circled his neck with her arms. "Will you take me upstairs?"

Other couples were ascending the staircase. Eddy, inclined by habit to follow the general example, escorted her to the first landing but hesitated. The girl pressed herself closer against his side. "You don't like me?"

Eddy mumbled and tried to push her away. The girl's grasp stiffened. He thoughtlessly applied a grip taught to him during his English apprenticeship. The girl screamed in pain and collapsed at his feet. He helped her up. "Sorry, why don't you go on, I'll see you later."

She gave him her room number, but he forgot it before he reached the ballroom again, deserted now but for Piasecki, chanting a lullaby and picking at his guitar. When the colonel saw Eddy he grinned furiously in a futile attempt to dispel the gloominess left by his song. "Have you exhausted the possibilities, lieutenant?"

"I think so, sir."

"I still have energy," Piasecki said, "let's destroy something."

There seemed to be a sufficiency of choice. Piasecki rolled an empty cognac bottle in the palm of his hands. "What's our target? Will that do?" He pointed at the invitingly gleaming skull of a servant diligently stacking dishes. "Shall we try Uncle Franz?"

"No," Eddy said, "Uncle Franz is usefully engaged." He looked around. "What do you think of that painting?"

The biblical king eyed Eddy disapprovingly from his ornate frame. Piasecki found his spectacles and walked over to the painting's corner. "But that joker looks like you. Are you going to maim yourself?"

"Why not, colonel?"

"As you like, the first throw is yours."

Whap. Eddy's beer bottle splintered against the wall. The old servant jumped and looked at the two men, his mouth gaping stupidly.

"My turn." Piasecki was ready. He assumed the attitude of an olympic discus thrower. *Whap*. Another miss. The Pole cursed in four languages. He leered at Uncle Franz. The old man attempted a bow and sidled to a door.

Eddy raised his voice. "My turn, colonel."

Piasecki, diverted by Eddy's shouting, allowed Uncle Franz to escape. "Yes, let him have it."

Eddy pivoted gracefully and let go of his projectile at the right moment this time, combining brute strength with centrifugal force. *Plop*.

"Right," the colonel shouted, "and about time too. As military men we do have to score every now and then."

Eddy's bottle was still in one piece, sticking out of the painting's torn linen. The young king's chest and the lower half of his face were covered by the bottle's obscene shape. The king's arrogant eyes remained focused on Eddy's face. A good shot.

Piasecki stumbled in Eddy's direction. "Lovely."

Eddy shook the offered hand and smiled gratefully.

"Would you like to join me in a spin of the town, lieutenant?"

"I'm sorry, sir, I would prefer to go to my room."

Eddy walked the colonel to his car in the courtyard and stood at attention while Piasecki's two-stroke DKW, still painted in the yellow greens of the Afrika Korps, started with the sound of drumsticks rattling on an empty can.

Eddy's memory failed to come up with the required information. Rather than highlighting psychological victories, it had thrown him back into an unfortunate moment, the meaning of which he could not grasp even today. There had been nothing wrong with the long-limbed, full-chested German woman who would no doubt have accompanied him in several hours of sexual play. Why had he refused his legal pleasure and, instead, wandered through the empty house, on stained floors, in between depressing debris. He tried to recall situations in which he had behaved more reasonably but found himself caught in another episode which again had to do with the antique painting in the villa's main room.

Uncle Franz came to disturb Eddy's late breakfast with a message from a Dutch visitor who inquired if there were any of his countrymen in the house. The intruder turned out to be a major, a small fidgety man who looked like a squirrel. Eddy remembered his manners and straightened up. "Lieutenant Sachs, major. At your service."

They were so close that their officer's sticks, clasped under their arms, clicked dryly against each other. The major seemed impressed by Eddy's correct and imposing bearing and stepped back. "Charles Vrieslander, lieutenant. I'm here on royal business. I'm looking for works of art stolen from the Netherlands and have been informed that there would be a Rembrandt here that belongs in the Rijksmuseum. Please allow me to look around."

"Certainly, major." Eddy glanced at the document that Major Vrieslander presented. *We, Queen Wilhelmina* . . . humm . . . *have charged Major Vrieslander* . . . humm . . . *has full authorization* . . . yes yes. There were certainly enough seals and signatures on the order.

The Rembrandt was found within minutes, in a corner of the hall where Onkel Franz had placed it, carefully wrapped in a piece of burlap.

"My God," the major said, "my dear sweet God, who did this? *Absalom* by Rembrandt, a priceless work of art. A beer bottle! Vandals, lieutenant, monsters of destruction. Would you please give me the name of whoever is to blame?"

Eddy came to attention briefly, then shrugged his shoulders. "A French guest, major, a general. I don't believe that there's anything you or I could do. Who, for instance, would we complain to? This house has been occupied by the British, but our commander is Polish. If regulations are strictly applied, you'd only be allowed to take the painting with his permission, but wouldn't that be waking sleeping dogs? Colonel Piasecki is asleep now, with a companion. He might not like to be disturbed. I seem to remember that he did drink quite a lot last night. I think that he hasn't noticed this painting and, should he be aware of its presence, might consider it to be a cheap copy of something. A Rembrandt, you say?"

Major Vrieslander pulled the beer bottle carefully out of the painting's linen. "Certainly. A Rembrandt, his portrait of Absalom. Just look at this mess. Well, never mind. I'll see if it can be restored. Do you need a receipt?"

"No, sir."

The major's car left the courtyard.

Eddy heard himself groan. The last memory had not been painful, so why was he suffering? Hadn't he taken care of the problem expediently? He became aware of the terrace around him and looked up to catch the waiter's eye. He could do with another drink. The waiter was nowhere in sight, but a woman in her early thirties, elegantly dressed and unaccompanied, happened to pass his table and smiled at him. Encouraged by his steady gaze she moved closer. Eddy hadn't quite freed himself from his daydreaming and was hardly aware of her presence. The woman bent down, displaying the deep shadow of her cleavage. Her voice was softly veiled. "Do you mind if I sit here?"

Eddy was firmly back in the present now. He didn't want the woman. He spoke loudly, and his harsh voice was even more noticeable because the conversation at the neighboring tables happened to subside at that moment.

"No. Please go away."

The woman staggered back and bumped into a table, glasses fell and broke. The old waiter appeared, muttering angrily.

A small man in a neat blazer and immaculately pressed flannel pants looked up from the far corner of the terrace and concentrated on Eddy's shape. "Damn," the man said softly, "the lieutenant who gave me the Rembrandt." He picked up his newspaper and placed money next to his unfinished drink.

Eddy saw Major Vrieslander and thought the dapper figure, now leaving the terrace, looked vaguely familiar.

Eddy, twenty-six years old, now carried the status of an ex-spy and inactive reserve officer with the rank of captain, distinctions which did not contribute to his present self-image. Only his training and experience mattered, and he was fond of seeing himself as an adventurer searching for something out of the ordinary. The world, he mused every morning while shaving, was still ready to offer him just about anything. But how to accept the bounty extended by circumstances? How to select?

There were the minor gifts, of course, like women and liquor. He ambled about, from pleasant pub to shadowed terrace, taking time to study the slow change of color on the trees and water birds gently bobbing on the canals. He strolled past the floating flower market and spent long hours in secondhand bookstores. There was also the nightlife that Amsterdam once again made available, and he shared his BMW and well-filled wallet with old friends or acquaintances he ran into in bars. No real opportunities opened up until he met two of his former theater school professors, who wanted to know what their promising student had been up to since he disappeared.

Eddy told them, first in general, then in detail, recreating the major scenes of his spectacular war years in the smoky space of a genever-scented bar. He acted out himself and the other main characters; he became the nervous pilot, the bronchitis-ridden general, the commando guerrillas on the Cornish coast, the dead fascist mayor, and the German detectives he had killed. He also impersonated Onkel Franz, Paul Kroll, and a number of the German women who had performed so well at the villa on the Kleine Alster.

"Whores?"

"They would never take money, we recruited them from high society."

"So how were they paid?"

"With suitable gifts, whatever we happened to have too much of at that moment."

"Attractive?"

"Oh, very," Eddy said enthusiastically, "lewd, willing, ready to fit into the conqueror's dream, overready sometimes, but one could forgive them their weakness."

"How fascinating, tell us more," the professors begged him.

"Shall I begin at the beginning?"

"If you please."

Eddy's hand formed exaggerated female shapes in the bar's dense atmosphere. "Listen to this then. I've just arrived in Germany, I'm on the periphery of Hamburg, in between villages that have been bombed into the ground and are still smoking. I'm lost. Next to me is a sergeant of the Dutch military police, a giant of a man."

The professors smiled encouragingly.

"A yokel and he got me lost. The fellow just drives on and on until I make him stop to ask for directions. Two attractive girls in their early twenties happen to be on the sidewalk. The sergeant asks them for the way. He puts out his arm and calls them." Eddy swept an ashtray from the counter. "Sorry. But those girls just keep on walking. We accelerate a little and catch up with them again. The sergeant repeats his request."

"We are getting somewhere," whispered one of the professors.

"Please don't interrupt me. Those girls just keep on walking."

"Right, right, right," the other professor said and licked his lips. "Oh, I can see it all."

55

"And they say something to each other, something negative or insulting, about us. We don't hear what they say but we can sense the meaning from their attitudes. Dutch cheeseheads, or something of the sort. And the military police sergeant says, 'Lieutenant, can I please?' And I say, 'But of course, sergeant, do what you have to do.' And he gets out. And . . ." Eddy paused, "pulls his gun."

"Those dames keep on walking, right?" the first teacher said, for Eddy had lost the thread of his tale or relived the scene so intensely that he had forgotten his audience.

"Right. The sergeant fires at the sun, with his big forty-five. A Browning. *Wham*."

"And then?"

"A sight to behold," Eddy said, "I had never seen anything like it. An all-time first. Those bitches, I'm telling you, they're quite attractive, not at all your farm types, elegant really, German women are often quite elegant, in a sexy way somehow, right, those bitches just stop, with their legs wide apart, seem to stiffen up, and . . ."

"And? And?"

"*Piss*," Eddy said, "no other word for it. You can't say they were relieving themselves, or urinating, or something like that, no, they were pissing. Like horses. Like pregnant mares. Thick foamy bubbly streams. Unbelievable. Well, believable of course, because there it was, splashing on the cobblestones. One moment pure arrogance, and the next, at the slightest aggression . . . that sergeant firing at the sky, there wasn't the whining of a bullet, just a big bang . . . a complete submission . . . pure fear of death."

He held up his glass. The bartender made the gin jar gurgle. "Your very good health. Yes, that was quite a spectacle."

"So did they point out the way after that?"

"Sure."

"And," the other professor asked, "did you, eh, sort of grab them afterward, to punish them I mean?"

Eddy struck a less victorious pose. "I've often thought of that since, for I didn't. The sergeant took them into the bushes and

56

suggested that I should join him. I did go to have a look because he stayed for a while. When I saw him he had ravaged one and was working on the other. Exciting in a way, but primitive. Even so . . ."

Eddy told other tales but the pointing-the-way story seemed to be the highlight of the evening. The professors agreed that Eddy's talent had ripened. They promised an introduction to the theater and kept their word. Eddy was on the stage within a week, portraying a mentally tortured German officer who returned to occupied Amsterdam, the scene of his crimes, and after much suffering, resolved his problems by committing suicide onstage. The Dutch audience loved it. Eddy was noticed by the critics and by women who waited for him nightly at the stage door. In due time the Ministry of Culture also paid attention and provided him with a grant to study at the Berlin School of Acting. Although he wasn't a star, Eddy was doing well. As his income was limited and unsteady he chose to live with a woman who, no longer young, was prepared to spend most of her considerable income to keep Eddy in a style that conformed to his fantasies. He drove her Italian sports car and wore tailor-made British suits.

She was Jewish and the idea of following him to Berlin made her come down with a sudden asthma attack.

"I don't think I can come with you," she wheezed.

Eddy had no reply; he had never meant to take her with him.

"Will you come and visit me?" she asked.

"I might not be back for a while."

He never saw the lady again.

PART II

West Berlin, 1955

The movie director's mustache drooped sadly beneath watery blue eyes magnified by heavy spectacles. His bald head glistened in the strong lights of the set. He wiped his hands on the dirty jersey which hung down to his knees. His flabby cheeks shook. "No, no, no. Cut."

Eddy put the gun down; the young girl, a hostage he was attempting to subdue, sneaked away in the direction of a cola machine.

"That's right," the movie director said, "more sugar. You're too chubby for the part already."

The girl scowled. "What's wrong now?"

"There you go again, flashing your teeth. I want you to threaten her. Sneer, drool a little, anticipate the sadistic thrill! You're going to violate the poor little thing, not accompany her to a ball. Oh, what's the use?"

"Shall we try again?"

The director looked at his watch. "No, I've had enough. Tomorrow is off, we all need a break."

Eddy was washing the make-up off his face. "I feel fine."

"I don't, I'm going boating tomorrow."

"Where?"

"On the Spree."

Eddy passed the towel. "Don't stray too far. The Russians shot

61

a man there yesterday, he was in a canoe with his kids. They apologized I hear."

"Who cares? Good night, Eddy."

"Good night, Hans."

The girl was fourteen but well formed, as she had pointed out to him before. She had painted her eyes while Eddy watched her pronounced bottom wiggle in tight slacks.

She smiled. "Give me a ride?"

"Sure, you live close by, don't you?"

"Not to my home, to yours."

"No, I'll drop you off where you live."

She pouted. "I've never seen your place, Judy says it's great."

Eddy swung himself into his open Citroën and pushed the passenger door open for her. "Get in, but you're only going around the corner."

She was doing her best to imitate Lauren Bacall. "What has Judy got that I haven't?"

Eddy grinned. "The right number of years. If you weren't fourteen I'd go for you."

The girl's voice shot up to its normal pitch. "You think I'm okay?"

"You bet."

He drove her to her door and got out. He opened her door. He even kissed her cheek. It wouldn't do to upset her; they still had several scenes to shoot and he didn't intend to give Hans a harder time than the director deserved.

Eddy drove on, admiring the cityscape whenever traffic lights interfered with his progress. He sang off key, "Berlin loves me, I'm Berlin's baby," adding happy "pom-poms" and lilting the words. The ditty fitted his mood. It was popular at the time, but he couldn't remember the rest of the words. He nodded at the gaunt tower of the partly destroyed Kaiser Wilhelm Church, pointing accusingly at a heaven that a mere ten years ago had held countless thousands of allied airplanes offloading their daily supply of steel-cased explosives. He registered the smooth shape of the new church next to the solitary tower, a modern dome that once again sheltered the religious. He also watched the crowd that still amazed him, ever since the days when he had first tried to get used to his new environment. An old woman in a black torn coat shuffled past, bent in her memory of total disaster, being overtaken by trim secretaries in tweed skirts and striped silk blouses. Imported laborers, shoddily suited, hurried to snackbars to feed quickly before rushing to second jobs, taking the city for granted, only intent on fattening the checks they sent home to Morocco or Turkey. Smart managers or lone self-employed entrepreneurs ambled about, doing multiplication sums in their heads while they tried to remember where they had parked their Porsches. The city's profit was increased by the lavish side-benefits the central government shelled out daily, encouraging the citizens to stay and keep this showpiece of democracy going, the fortress flung farthest into the hostile East. Everyone knew that the Russians were oiling their war machinery, waiting for a shift in the balance of power, watching from the deadly ring that embraced the city, but nobody dared to show concern. They were all Berlin's babies.

To be throttled in the cradle, Eddy thought happily, while I sneak away. The threat of war and conquest, so painfully ignored by Berlin's bourgeoisie, added to his pleasure. War would provide fun again, even more than the joy he was now extracting from the studio's make-believe. One has to live with the times. War gives a kick; peace, steady wealth, in the form of luxury that he was now earning himself. He owned his car and could easily afford the high rent of a five-room apartment overlooking the famous Tiergarten, furnished in his own choice of chrome and leather bought on time payments. His mind flew high and his body was in fine trim. He was still reading his psychology books, and worked out in a gymnasium run by one of Hitler's special troopers, noble Otto, one of the heroes who liberated Mussolini from his jail perched on a mountain top. Otto von Kirst had become a friend. Eddy also had another, even more affluent friend. Whenever Paul Kroll flew out from Hamburg, Eddy met the ex-Obersturmbahnführer at the Tempelhof airport and entertained him in style. Kroll came for the high life, dinner in an out-of-the-way restaurant displaying Michelin Guide stars, a girlie show, and a visit to a villa in the Grünewald where Berlin's best prostitutes entertained him and his friend at ten marks per minute, all desires satisfied, tips not welcome.

"I hear you have a friend from Hamburg who visits sometimes," Otto said. "You might introduce us."

"I might."

Eddy preferred to be mysterious; secrets improved the mask he wore when he was with Otto. He did not intend to bring the two men together. They were too different, and he preferred to have each one to himself.

Splendid Otto, who liked to wear a cape over his close-fitting clothes, looked somewhat like Dracula and was, Eddy sometimes thought, perhaps truly evil. It was a pity Otto didn't like being an actor; director Hans would have done well with him. Otto ran a sideline, drugs, pushing them on the very wealthy via his henchmen. He wanted Eddy to deal too — movie stars make many contacts.

"No."

"Why not?" Otto snarled softly. "Heroin is money. You spend a lot of it."

"No."

"Pah," Kroll said, slouched on a couch in the Grünewald brothel. "It's only cocaine. Stuff gives you a glow."

"No thanks."

Kroll raised a tempting hand. "Won't get you into the subconscious, I wouldn't take it if it did. Bad dreams should be avoided, coke brings out what you learned in the past, it steers you away from what you wish to forget."

Eddy, once his charm was scratched away, could be quite forbidding. He stared at Kroll coldly. "All right, all right," Kroll said lazily, "pour him another drink, honey." Kroll was also riding high; the Free Eagle in Hamburg, although not supplying the forbidden pleasures, brought in a steady trickle of gold, and he also owned a car agency with a steadily increasing turnover. Kroll could afford to be pudgy; his large frame supported a lot of extra weight easily. He rolled along.

Eddy constructed a theory that fitted both Kroll and Otto. They each contributed to his aura. Kroll represented German geniality, *Gemütlichkeit,* and Otto, destructive negativity. The German idea of being happy together was a boisterous, large concept, quite unlike the Dutch habit of linking arms for comfort. Eddy had always abhorred the Dutch. They were a small, fearful people, always huddling. The Germans, when joined, did things in a bigger way and weren't bothered by petty morals. They were likely to make big mistakes, of course, and he was glad he had chosen to fight against them, but the present was not the past. Kroll had turned out to be a great man. Eddy admired the way in which the once hopeless prisoner twisted fate, as he promised to do when he left the Röherstrasse jail. He felt secure with Kroll's motivation; the man was after money and what money could buy.

Eddy and Otto sprawled on Eddy's balcony, resting their eyes on the foliage surrounding the zoo below. It had been a hot day, but the famous Berlin air, freshened by its trip over eastern, lake-studded flatlands, had cooled already and was easy to breathe. Even Otto looked comfortable.

"What do you intend to achieve?" Eddy asked, pushing a decanter of chilled wine to his guest.

Otto growled.

"Pardon?"

"Freedom."

"Aren't we all free?"

The cadaverous man smacked his thin lips. "As free as they are down there." He pointed at panthers below, lolling on sun-warmed rocks behind a moat and high wall. "We Germans are caught by the Russians and types like you who come and stay and watch us for a while. The earth should have been ours. Now we're only allowed to be a buffer zone and fill our time by manufacturing useful supplies for the conquerors." Otto crouched in his chair.

He's like one of the panthers, Eddy thought. The panthers below were having an argument, leering at each other, swishing their tails in the sand. Gunfire roared in the distance. "It might all start again. You'll have another chance."

Otto leaned forward, listening to the evil rumble.

"You don't think so?" Eddy asked.

"No. For us it is over." Otto didn't finish his drink and left abruptly. Eddy watched him slouch to his car. The gloominess that pervaded the apartment hung on and later seemed to foreshadow a number of changes that affected his life from then on. Eddy lost his uninsured car in an accident, incurred a large debt, and spent considerable time in the hospital due to a burst appendix, during which time his apartment was burglarized. Director Hans, suffering from unclear mental disorders, lost ground. He solved his problem while cruising along Potzdamerstrasse in his Cadillac where he picked up two young men. He promised a merry evening in his house and provided it. They murdered him before they left. Eddy was now out of work. He tried other studios and was told there wasn't much doing. A good supply of younger and cheaper talent existed.

Eddy persisted but nothing turned up.

Late one night Eddy stood hunched on his balcony, fists dangling at his sides, frowning, concentrating to the bursting point. "What is this? Why aren't you listening to me? I won't wait any longer."

He didn't know who he was talking to, but whoever it was answered, via a third party. Eddy's telephone rang. A taped voice, so weak and broken that Eddy didn't recognize it until the speaker gave his name, begged him to come to where Unter den Linden crosses Friedrichstrasse, south corner, tomorrow, eleven A.M. sharp. "Get me out of here," the voice whispered. "You'll be paid well."

The tape clicked off; the phone went dead.

Eddy considered the proposition. The address was in East Berlin, the territory of the damned.

"Sure," he said to the unlistening phone.

66

East Berlin, 1960

The voice manifested itself again, embodied this time, but just as broken as it had sounded on tape. "Were you followed?"

"If I was, I must have shaken him off by now."

"Are you sure?"

"Positive."

"If they see us together, we are both in serious trouble."

"They won't," Eddy said impatiently. "Stop worrying, Rogier. Buy me some coffee, I've already spent most of the East marks they gave me at the checkpoint on taxis. What's with you?"

The man's skin was gray. His clothes looked like he had slept in the street. Eddy sipped the foul tasting coffee, waiting for his contact to speak. They had worked together in Holland, during the last and most hectic year of the war. Rogier was a dedicated communist then, ready to preach his creed at the drop of an empty cartridge, prattling about a new world of share and share alike. He had also been energetic and alert. Now he was a shadow, almost lamed by fatigue and fear. The cup rattled as Rogier replaced it on its cracked saucer. "I came here ten years ago, willing to work for them."

"Fool."

Rogier waved the insult away tiredly. "It was all different, it

67

took me a long time to see it, to give up what I had made myself believe."

"You turned all the way?"

"Oh yes."

"You were caught?"

For a moment Rogier's face was alive. "Not quite, I was trained well, I confessed in general, without mentioning details."

"They let you off?"

"For the time being." Rogier coughed. The sound made Eddy look up. "Are you ill?"

"A fever, it's been with me for a while. The cells here aren't too good."

Eddy pushed his clean handkerchief over the table. "Keep it. What do you want me to do?"

Rogier blew his nose carefully. "I know quite a bit and want to pass my information to the West. Western agents are scarce here, most have disappeared and I don't trust who're left. If you help me get back, I will sell what I own in Holland and retire, you can have half the proceeds."

"How much?"

Rogier coughed in the handkerchief. "Can't say exactly, enough I suppose."

"You have your family out here?"

"I divorced before I came out, my wife preferred socialism to communism. I thought she was too weak."

"Who took the tape across?"

"A friend, it's hard to make a direct telephone connection, I knew where you were, I even passed your address once to my former chief, were you ever approached by them?"

Eddy grinned. "So it was you? That was awhile back, I said I wasn't interested, I was doing too well. Why didn't your friend take you across?"

Rogier shrugged. "He is a cripple, he was given a pass to visit a dying sister. I need a professional."

Eddy watched sparse traffic passing the café; old-model cars, most of them prewar, endlessly repaired and repainted, flowed slowly past, directed by military-looking young policemen in new uniforms. A line of haggard women carrying paper bags waited patiently for a store to let them in. He looked back at Rogier. "You have a plan?"

"Yes. There's a building in the demarcation zone, its inhabitants will soon be moved out, but the process is delayed by red tape. I know people there and have timed the patrols. To the rear is a yard that leads to the stripped zone. The actual border consists of rolls of barbed wire, tied together. I have two pairs of good clippers. We can get across if we run at the right time and make our way through the wire quickly. I can't do it on my own, I'm not strong. I can help a little and keep watch while you work. There's some shadow there, cast by shrubs and a dead tree, we won't be clearly visible."

"I need money," Eddy said. "You'll have to pay me or I'll have to come after you later."

Rogier nodded. "I've always been trustworthy."

Eddy pushed his coffee away. "I have a tourist pass, it runs out tomorrow, we'll have to go tonight."

"We can pass the afternoon in the building, they haven't seen me go there. I'm no longer under surveillance. The secret police is overworked. I was put on parole, I go to check with them every day. I visited the office this morning."

Eddy smiled. "Let's go."

Eddy took a bus; Rogier walked. Eddy had memorized the directions, making Rogier repeat them slowly; he had no intention of being lost between concrete monuments decked with banners screaming slogans in red capitals. He had dressed down for the occasion, wearing nondescript pants and a workingman's jacket. He hadn't shaved and carried a plastic bag of Eastern German manufacture. While the bus was stopped a parade passed. Eddy held on to a frayed strap. He wondered whether the adventure was worth his while. Rogier should have valuable information, but the Dutch wouldn't pay much; it might be better if Rogier sold his secrets to the highest bidder. Eddy realized his risk; he had lived in Berlin long enough, read the papers, heard the stories. He couldn't afford to be caught; the enemy would never believe that he only meant to save an acquaintance, trained in the same Cornish spy school, and was selling his services for mere money.

The parade marched on, young men sang lustily and waved flags, trumpets blared, drums rattled. What did they believe in now? Prophet Marx? Archangel Lenin? Nothing had changed; the robots would waste their energy again, on an inane pursuit dictated by the erring voices of the dead. Different caps, same jackboots, better arms. The soldiers held Russian-made submachine guns, guaranteed not to fail even if dropped in the dirt. The communist craziness was more down to earth than the fascist; perhaps it was less bothered by intelligence; its power drive had to be primitive but worked better than the conflicting stupidities of Hitler's magic. The communist Reich was already several times the size of the Nazi state at its heyday. They'll be easier to outwit, Eddy thought, especially in the short run.

He met Rogier again in the crumbling building, divided into one-room apartments for the elderly. Rogier stared out of a window, watch in hand. "There's a motorbike patrol every ten minutes. There they come."

The bike, a light Czechoslovakian model with a two-stroke engine, puttered past. It looked new. The two soldiers riding it were still in their teens. Two young girls on the West side of the wire fence had stopped to peer across the wasteland. The soldiers waved at them. The girls turned away.

"It can be done," Rogier said. "There have been many escapes recently. Soon it will be impossible. They're planning a nine-foot wall, towers, electrical wires, dogs, a moat. Once the wall is up, only dreams can escape."

"It's a dream now," Eddy said. The innocent sound of the motorcycle died away in the distance. Sparrows twittered in the wire. An old woman with a scarf tied around her head came out to feel a pair of pants drying on a line. She smiled tiredly before turning back to the house.

"She's all right," Rogier said.

Eddy touched Rogier's shoulder. "You take a nap, I'll stay here, maybe I'll get some ideas. We can cut the worst of the wire and throw boards over the rest; there might be some around."

Eddy found boards in the basement; they were old but still useful. The old woman came out again and helped him stack the boards against the house. She worked efficiently. "I know the two boys who do the evening patrol. The one with the red hair might be helpful. He would like to go himself; his father is a party member, he hates him. He wants to go to the promised land to sleep with the lovely girls he is seeing on Western television and across the fence."

"And the other one?"

She shook her head slowly. "I'm not sure. He is a good boy, here he'll go to waste. Maybe he wants to go too, I told him he should. My own sons left years ago, when it was still easier."

"Did they go through here?"

"No. This is a risky route, but everything is dangerous now."

"They might blame you if we make it."

Her false teeth clacked as she chuckled. "I don't care anymore, I'm almost eighty." She took him to a communal kitchen on the first floor and cut bread, smearing the slices thinly with margarine. Eddy had remembered to bring some provisions out of West Berlin and shared his sausage and cheese with her. He enquired about Rogier.

"He came with my husband, they met in the street. My husband doesn't care who he talks to and what he says, he is old too."

"He took the tape across?"

She nodded, smiling at the taste of the cheese. He gave her the rest of his supplies, a can of sardines and a small flask of schnapps. She offered her bed and Eddy lay down, dozing off now and then.

Eddy and Rogier left just after dark. Eddy worked quickly cutting a foot of wire, then arranging the boards. He told Rogier to crawl across. Their timing was correct but the patrol came early. Rogier froze; Eddy flattened himself against the wire rolls. He had transferred the mayor's gun from his fly to his side pocket and brought it out. It was fully loaded again, with cartridges bought on the West Berlin black market. The motorbike rode past them. Eddy was getting up when it made a sharp turn and came back. The soldiers had noticed irregular shapes but didn't seem too suspicious. Their snubnosed weapons were still slung across their backs as they got off the bike.

Eddy's revolver was up. His cold whisper cut across the wasteland. "Stay where you are. Drop your guns." The soldiers obeyed.

"Kill them," Rogier said softly.

Eddy didn't think he should. The shots would trigger off an alarm somewhere; more soldiers would arrive, spraying their fire from several points.

"Come with us," he said softly. "The boards will hold, you'll be free."

The red-haired soldier moved forward; the other seemed frozen to the ground.

Eddy could hear Rogier move away from him. He circled the soldiers, picked up the submachine guns and flung them across the wire. The red-haired boy was following Rogier.

"What about you?" Eddy asked the other.

"No. I don't want my family to suffer."

Rogier was safe; the red-haired boy was almost there. A Russian-made vehicle carrying four men came roaring toward them. "The control," the waiting soldier said. "Get away."

Eddy jumped on the boards and ran; they crackled and broke under his feet but his momentum kept him going. He leaped the last three feet; as he cleared the wire and rolled over on his shoulder, he heard the sound of bullets tearing into flesh and was surprised it wasn't his own. "Keep down," Rogier yelled. An American jeep turned up on the western side. The G.I.'s faced the East Germans; for a few seconds weapons were raised on both sides, then discipline prevailed. Each party knew better than to openly provoke an incident. An ambulance arrived, called by the German vehicle's radio. The body of the boy-soldier shot by his own people was picked up by stone-faced attendants and carried to the van on a stretcher. The red-haired boy staggered to Rogier, gasping for air. Rogier held the crying soldier's hand. "There's nothing you can do. Accept what happened and live on. You're on the *right* side now."

Preaching again, Eddy thought as he brushed himself off. His gun was back in his pocket. He had an opportunity to maneuver it into his fly while being taken to a barracks for interrogation. The American border guards released him once his identity was established.

Rogier stayed with the military and was flown to Allied Headquarters the next day. A week later a check arrived, considerably more than Eddy expected. It paid his debts and allowed him to live on in comfort for more than a year. A new studio supplied some bit parts, and he found temporary work as a stunt man, where he had to turn over cars and dangle from a helicopter. Then the contracts ran out again, forcing him to employ an agent who secured him odd jobs from time to time.

"You know," the agent said one morning, "maybe you shouldn't bother to come in so often. I have your number and I can drop you a note."

Eddy turned back.

"Wait," the agent said, "I may have something right now. An importer I know is looking for a model. There isn't much cash in it, but the work is easy enough. Would you like to model French-style, Taiwan-made suits for older men? All you have to do is dye your hair gray."

Eddy flew to Hamburg the same day, without canceling his rent or saying good-bye to anyone. He carried what he owned.

"So you're stuck?" Kroll's large leather-upholstered desk chair turned soundlessly on its heavy axle. "That's good. I'll get you unstuck again, for that's what I promised to do long ago."

His bulging eyes rested on Eddy's tall body, reclining easily in another leather seat on the visitor's side of the desk. Eddy's feet were on a small table. His arms rested on the chair's sides. He was smiling.

"You don't look stuck," Kroll said accusingly.

"But I am."

"What can I get you? Money? A job?"

"A camel and a rifle," Eddy said.

Kroll grunted.

"Or a Chinese junk, a cigar, and a load of white slave girls."

Kroll unfolded a plastic envelope and sprinkled a little white powder on the palm of his hand. He looked at Eddy but remembered in time. "A drink?"

Kroll telephoned and a waiter from his bar downstairs brought whiskey. Kroll waited for the man to leave his office and raised his glass. "Your health. So I can finally repay you. It shouldn't please me, for one doesn't like to see a friend in trouble."

"I'm not in trouble," Eddy said brightly. "I told you what I am, I'm stuck. I've run out of thoughts."

"You still have some," Kroll corrected. "The junk? The camel you mentioned just now?"

"No good," Eddy said. "I haven't got the age to go with that. Daydreams without substance. I took the wrong turn somewhere and I can't even remember where and when it was. Berlin seemed a good idea, maybe it was for a while."

"But you need money."

"Yes."

"And a job?"

"Yes," Eddy said. "I'm broke, you're right that far."

"I'm right all the way." Kroll shifted uneasily in his seat. "And my ass burns. Hemorrhoid trouble. I sit here for hours on end and feel my ass burn, while I dream."

"Of what?" Eddy asked politely.

Kroll watched his fingers — soft sausages, neatly spread on the glass plate on his desk. "Of my tank, I see it again, the way it looked just before it ran out of gas and ammunition in the Ukranian mud. In my dream I keep on driving it, and it slithers on frozen snow. Sometimes the dream changes — I fly a plane, make it skim over tree tops before strafing the enemy. Pah."

"Pah?" Eddy asked.

Kroll's poetry broke off. "What sort of a job do you want?" He crumpled the little plastic envelope and dropped it into the wastebasket. "Would you like me to connect you? I would rather buy from you than from my present contact."

"Push dope? No."

"You want to work for me? Run the Free Eagle once in a while so that I can get away?"

"Not really."

Kroll frowned. "What else can I offer? Would you care to sell my cars? I can fire the man who works for me now. I've specialized in sports cars, little jobs women like to buy. You might like the variety in clientele and do well in different ways."

"I'd still be stuck. I prefer to move about."

Kroll grinned. "How much cash do you need right now?"

"A few thousand would be very nice."

Kroll wrote a check. "Would you like a car too?"

"Yes, but don't put yourself out."

They drove to Kroll's agency and Eddy picked out a used convertible.

"It's yours," Kroll said. "But we aren't even yet. Come back in a few days, maybe I'll have found the right vacancy by then. Would you like to show tourists around Italy?"

Within a week Eddy began to cart loads of the curious and travel-fevered about, in a new-model touring bus, comfortably leaning back in his soft seat next to the upright driver, monotonously explaining through a microphone. The tourists were usually Japanese, which he preferred them to be, for their knowledge of English was rudimentary and he could improvise freely, for the benefit of the driver who was not unintelligent.

Together they engaged in vaudeville, finding new explanations for why the Tower of Pisa leans over, the murkiness of Venetian canals, and other phenomena they had to present to their audience. Eddy recited these theories, drawing puzzled bows from the tourists and snickers from the driver. There were other diversions, such as private sightseeing with his driver-friend and occasional seductions — some female in the bus always looked better than the others. Eddy was fifty-six now, but he had aged gracefully. He still had most of his hair and only needed eyeglasses for small print. Outward change was slow.

His routine kept him going. There was always the next trip and its preparations and a fresh crowd to lug about. He slept in luxury hotels, ate good meals, and even enjoyed himself at times, mostly when he returned to museums in his free time. Certain examples of modern art fascinated him, for no apparent reason, and he would spend minutes on end lost in thought in front of a painting, and come back to it again later.

He had also a hometown, Hamburg, where Kroll waited, and although Eddy usually limited their meetings to a shared lunch, or just a few drinks at the Free Eagle's bar, the idea that he wasn't alone was helpful.

Of any inward change Eddy had little intimation, but some hints would emerge at odd moments, such as when he admired a meticulous scene painted by Paul Delvaux, depicting a naked woman sprawled on a red velvet couch. She was surrounded by skeletons, calmly observing the model's beauty, and an open window behind the woman's form added depth to the vision, making it spread to the horizon, opening up a vast vista dotted by other undressed ladies and more skeletons. Eddy, caught by the artist's relentless imagination, could not get away and spent an hour in the museum, worrying a custodian who suspected the rapt visitor of wanting to damage a work of art.

The next day another ray, mysteriously loosened from within his deeper mind, shed some light on the turn his fate would take. Eddy was waiting in a dentist's office and picked up a book of cartoons. One of the collection's crudely drawn picture-stories showed a little man sporting a long white beard, happily out for a walk, with the sun in the sky, birds singing, and rabbits gamboling about his feet. Failing to pay attention, he fell into a hole. At the bottom of the hole his devil waited. The ensuing fight was terrifying. The devil went all out, swinging his prey around by the beard, kicking him in the genitals, tweaking his nose, jumping on his belly. Little clouds emerging from the old man's head described his thoughts. The old man was desperately thinking of defense, drawing on the experience of a long and varied life, working out a way of being rid of his tormentor.

The devil multiplied himself, and attacked his victim from all sides. It was clear that the old man couldn't last much longer.

Then the answer popped up. *I must*, the old man thought while he was being trampled into the ground of the hole's bottom, *hang loose*.

Only one devil was left, the original demon. The old man was on his feet in good shape, and the devil, exhausted, leaned against the frame that held the picture. He pretended to be bored and poked between his fangs with a long nail.

"You lost," the old man said.

"Don't tell me how you won," the devil answered, dropping to his knees, begging for mercy. "If you do, it's all over with me."

"I only hung loose."

The last picture of the cartoon was a repeat of the first. The old man sauntered in the field again; the sun was in the sky; birds were singing; rabbits frolicked.

Eddy was called into the dentist's office. The treatment was painful. I must get away from this, Eddy thought, I must hang loose.

The drill whined on, approaching a nerve. There was no pain when it struck.

PART III

Rome, 1976

The Jumbo's gleaming mass began its descent in a sky whose gun-metal sheen was fading into the hollow blackness of night. Within moments a dignified and uninflected female voice would request that passengers extinguish all smoking material.

Some ash from the stub of Charles Vrieslander's cigarette spilled on his little round paunch pushing above stylish trousers. He shook his head abruptly when the stewardess offered him a final drink. She favored him with a smile and snapped his tray into the recess of the chair ahead. No more liquor on this trip, he thought. He'd had enough by now, especially during the last few days in Bogotá. The plateau supporting the Colombian capital is nine thousand feet high and its thin air has an unpleasant influence on visitors. Those who can handle half a bottle in Florence should watch themselves after the third glass in Bogotá. His stomach felt as if it had been filled with molten lead, and his intestines were inflated with the filthy stenches of South America — proved every time his behind, forced by sudden turbulence, left the seat. Thanks to the efficient air-conditioning his foul gas now polluted the stratosphere. The cramps hadn't subsided yet, and he had a bad headache.

The little man reclining in his first-class seat's luxurious embrace sighed. His expensive surroundings did not cheer him. The seductive radiance of stewardesses moving gracefully through the aisle seemed no more to him than unappealing blobs of color that wouldn't stay put. His dulled brain failed to conjure up a pleasant image. Even his Ferrari, hesitantly and perhaps helpfully projecting itself on his mind's screen, depressed him. He defined the car parked in the catacombs under Rome's airport as a useless vehicle that couldn't be satisfactorily repaired even by master mechanics. Its speedometer's cable would be clicking again and irritate him all the way to Empoli, to his money-draining villa, and to Viola.

Viola! Charlie smiled for the first time since he had left Italy six days earlier. Viola — a hyperactive sprite, hard to deal with, spoiled and despicable in many ways, and like all kept women a professional faker of emotion and orgasms. But she loved older men, especially if they resembled her father, and Charlie, according to Viola, looked very much like her father, although, she claimed, he was better equipped. Her aberration suited him well, from the day that he married her eight years before when she was eighteen years old and attractive but in no way as physically perfect as now. She was a splendid addition to his collection of valuable objects and, because she had the added virtue of being alive, was also useful — able to charm the clients who bought his art. So he had done something right after all, he thought. Why, there had even been a notable period when he had thought himself in love with her. In love, really . . .

He shrugged carefully, so that his behind did not leave the chair, and pushed the curtain away. Rome's tiara of lights flickered their welcome, but not as warmly as when he returned from previous trips. He knew many people down there, business connections who had thought enough of him to make the effort to pronounce his name correctly. Had thought. The past. He scowled. Rome's lights, no matter how dazzling and alluring they were, only outlined a complicated snare for Charles Vrieslander in his present position. His scowl froze while he imagined the reception the jackals would be preparing.

The first to pounce would be Verleur — a bald and aging queen who ran the Florence branch of the Netherlands General

Bank. "Welcome, Mr. Vrieslander, you *are* here to make your payment? You *are* aware that a *substantial* amount of accumulated interest is due on your mortgage?"

How much was fifteen percent cumulative over a year? Charlie's mind entangled itself in the calculation and he gave up. The queen was still yapping anyway. "You realize that if you cannot settle immediately we will be required to foreclose on the collateral . . . and yank it from under your farting asshole? Your villa, Mr. Vrieslander? Complete with assorted items? You *are* aware that the same goes for the Jaguar, and the Chevrolet Camaro, and that ridiculous little toy of yours, the Ferrari with the clicking speedometer cable? But do not despair, Mr. Vrieslander, for without your own transportation you'll qualify, in view of your age, for a discount on the streetcar. It'll only be three hundred lire to Empoli from here, and if the streetcar should chance to break down, as it frequently does I hear, you'll be free to walk. You remember how to do that, walk?" A sarcastic bastard, banker Verleur. Banker? A penny-ante teller in drag, a flunky relaying messages from gods back home. In Dutch, too. Why was he dealing with a Dutch bank anyhow? Italian bankers were easier to put off, and wore decent suits as well.

He would have to stall Verleur somehow. Would he palm that imitation Modigliani off on him, the elongated profile of a young street girl squinting at her ravisher? Or maybe that small unsigned Vermeer would do the trick? Accomplish the deal in his usual straightforward manner? "Quite candidly, Mr. Verleur, the provenance of this Vermeer is not impeccable. The experts do not agree among themselves and I tend to agree with their hesitations. But so much is certain, if the master himself did not paint this landscape then one of his close disciples surely did. Shall we say two thousand dollars, in view of our special relationship?" Charlie stopped scowling; the faker in Milano had only charged him a thousand. But there were other problems.

He moved inadvertently and reached, nostrils flaring, for the air nozzle above him. His intestines had to be coated with Colombian mold. Or did he have worms? He waited for the vapors to

83

waft away. Verleur was only problem number one and perhaps he could take care of him for a while. Now problem two, however ...

"Ladies and gentlemen. Because there are too many airplanes wishing to land, we have been placed in a holding pattern. I estimate that we will be delayed for some ten minutes."

Charlie frowned irritably. Couldn't that pilot keep his trap shut? He concentrated again. Problem number two: a check made out in Charlie's name for $185,000, mailed a month ago in Asunción, Paraguay. Where was that check?

Yes, what had happened to it? That money was his, but he didn't have it. Maybe he would never have it. Had some crook cashed that bit of paper, proving with false I.D. that he was Charles K. Vrieslander? Not impossible at all. A criminal had swiped the greenbacks off the counter, maybe sharing the loot with the teller. Surely the amount of money was large enough to motivate two con men to collaborate. Would, at this very same moment, two unhealthy looking South American ex-bank clerks be toasting each other in an expensive Mediterranean nightclub at his expense? Charlie shut his eyes tightly in agony. Why the hell hadn't he accepted Herr Hulsow's personal check? Couldn't Hulsow be trusted for any amount? Good old Hulsow, Charlie's friend dating back to the merry faraway war years when Hulsow was still called Schink and held a high Nazi rank.

Charlie had earned that $185,000 diligently and honestly. Herr Hulsow required some ambience for his new hotel in the Seychelles. Charlie supplied him with the requested material: a collection of expensive art centered around a rare Khmer stone Buddha. Hulsow, as always, was prepared to pay on delivery.

But no. "A banker's check, please, Hulsow, drawn on your bank in Paraguay, and to be airmailed, unregistered." Charlie didn't want to be caught again. The Italian customs had already grabbed him once. They went through his pockets and found checks.

"Would Signore Dottore Vrieslander kindly explain how he managed to carry that much in foreign funds if he only declared a laborer's income to the Italian income tax authorities?"

That little joke had cost him a fortune in bribes. It shouldn't happen again. Charlie now brought his money in through the regular mail.

But the check didn't arrive in the regular mail; the check didn't arrive at all. The Asunción bank, alerted by cable, promised to investigate matters. As if anybody in Paraguay ever investigated anything except secretaries' underwear.

Had he really lost that money? "No!" Charlie groaned aloud.

The stewardess who had sat down next to him for the plane's landing smiled empathetically. Charlie bared his teeth in response. "Go fuck the pilot." He had spoken Dutch but the tone of his voice was cutting and the girl looked away sheepishly.

Problem number three: von Wittenberg's stroke. How could Freiherr Hans August von Wittenberg-Pritzwalk have the audacity to suffer a stroke?

While the 747, obeying her computers, nosed down faultlessly, Charlie grumbled. How could it be that the all-powerful Nazi general, before whom western Holland had once trembled, could have changed into his present shape? It couldn't really be true that von Wittenberg, ruler of Charlie's universe, the protector, the friend, was now a helpless old man, in the grasping hands of a priestly doctor performing magical rites in a Bogotá medical clinic.

But it was true. The fallen god could no longer defend Charlie's interest, no longer recognized his friends and loyal retainers. The palatial gates of Colombian marijuana growers, Peruvian coca farmers, Venezuelan oil barons, and Brazilian and Argentine generals manipulating developing funds originating in Europe and the United States were now closed to art dealer Vrieslander. No more deals, and South America was Charlie's best market.

He had waited unsuspectingly for von Wittenberg in the winter garden of Bogotá's Hotel Continental, smiling quietly between flowering tropical plants, certain that the curving line of his luck was about to surge upward again.

Surely he could rightfully have thought that? How could he have expected his guardian angel to show himself as a shuffling wreck, supporting his wasted frame on crutches, wrapped in a fur

85

coat while the temperature was close to ninety? What had happened to von Wittenberg's face? Why was the left eye, stupid and round, riveted on Charlie and the other almost closed? Von Wittenberg had to make a supreme effort to remember who Charlie was. Von Wittenberg's memory was paralyzed by the fear of death.

Charlie hurried through his cheerful greetings to lead to describing his pressing problem. Von Wittenberg wasn't listening. Yet Charlie's story wasn't uninteresting, especially because he intended to tell the truth — how he had been buying gold, every available ounce, first with his own resources and then with borrowed money supplied by the Mafia. Gold was going up in 1976, and up again, and higher still. He had been buying at $150 and meant to sell at $200. Only $200 never came. The gamblers were waiting, holding their breath; the Mafia was waiting too. When the price oscillated around $175 and came down again, the Mafia lost their patience. Two quiet young men dressed in tapered sharkskin suits rode down the driveway of the Empoli villa and parked their immaculate white Guzzi motorcycles, one on each side of Charlie's impressive granite steps. They pushed the visors of their helmets up and smiled softly.

"A message from Capo Filippo."

Charlie bowed.

"The Capo would like to see his two million again." The speaker, the more handsome and larger of the two, smiled apologetically. "Capo Filippo isn't talking about lire. If this was about lire we wouldn't bother you. The matter involves dollars. You have a few days."

The motorcyclists waited.

"A week," Charlie said. "Would that be all right?"

The motorcyclists checked their watches and read the date and the time aloud, harmonizing their melodious voices. "One week, Signore Vrieslander."

The price of gold eased further down and passed the level at which Charlie had brought. Even so he paid when the motorcyclists returned, regardless of the fact that he had now lost his entire capital. He appreciated the Capo's allowing him to live and made an effort to continue to do so in his customary style. Bills kept on flowing in, however, stacking themselves in his solid copper letter box. Viola was still visiting her hairdresser and needed new clothes constantly. The villa consumed large quantities of electricity. Charlie ate shrimp and *escargot*, soaking them as usual in cognac. Credit became hard to obtain and Mr. Verleur's grating voice no longer minced words.

"So, you see, dear Herr General, I am more or less bankrupt, but no matter for I'm sure you can help me out for a time. Considering my faithful services of the past and the truth that I have never, never, betrayed you, not even in my thoughts, and because you are the living example of everything that I admire, I now beg you on my pink knees to please expedite my return to Easy Street."

That's how Charlie had intended to phrase his request, in sincerity, humility, and faith.

Von Wittenberg's enormous eye stayed fixed on his nail-chewing visitor, sitting forlornly in a large cane chair stuck between an exuberant display of tropical flowers on the hotel's glass-covered veranda.

"Yes," said von Wittenberg after a long pause, "this holy priest will surely cure me. I have come to Bogotá to experience the grace of the padre's spiritual aura. Many men my age owe their lives to the good care of Padre Gomez. I will meet with him tomorrow morning. Surely you are acquainted with Padre Gomez's reputation?"

"Sir?"

Charlie turned.

"The airplane has landed. Please make sure not to forget your personal belongings."

The stewardess, worried that the nervous and mumbling passenger would not be able to find his way to the airport, accompanied Charlie to the customs barrier.

The officials pressed the keyboard of their computer: V-r-i-e-s-l-a-n-d-e-r. The machine answered. The men smiled.

"Very well, dottore. Do you have anything to declare?"

"Nothing."

"Are you sure?"

"Yes."

"Please step this way."

Once again, with no way to escape. The officials made him undress. One of the officers even stooped so low as to peer into the dottore's anus. Charlie made a superior effort to restrain himself, to no avail. The official staggered backward.

"Please be good enough to open your satchel."

Two bottles appeared.

"You are only allowed to bring in one bottle of spirits."

Charlie offered the forbidden bottle.

"Attempting to bribe an officer is a crime, signore, you are causing us more trouble."

Charlie produced a banknote of a high denomination and placed it reverently next to the bottle.

Bottle and note disappeared.

The Ferrari's speedometer cable clicked louder than ever. The thick traffic that kept the small car in its solid grip seemed more tangled than he had experienced before. By cutting across the sidewalk here and there and ignoring traffic lights, Charlie succeeded in liberating himself and eventually reaching the autostrada where he joined an interminable column of heavy trucks moving hesitantly at minimal speed. He breathed partly burned oil for the next ten kilometers.

Why was he still toiling away if the scales refused to tip the other way? Hadn't he always represented von Wittenberg's interests according to the highest possible standards? Could the general, even in his present predicament, forget the list of Jewish art dealers' addresses that Charlie submitted in 1941, well before the Gestapo was ready to pounce? And later, when the Reich had disintegrated, hadn't Charlie fed the Odessa line conscientiously with works of art cleverly torn from the grabbing hands of the Allied occupation forces?

And now, now that he, in his turn, wanted to ask for a favor, now . . . Charlie cursed so violently that he hurt his throat.

Padre Gomez! A Colombian quack was allowed to suck the Freiherr's wealth, drain it completely, while Charlie fell back into the fires of hell.

The trucks finally moved and the strada opened out. The Ferrari jumped as Charlie's foot pressed the tiny accelerator, until the car purred at 160 kilometers an hour. He nearly missed the off-ramp to Empoli but managed to bring the sports car into an almost ninety-degree turn.

Viola was waiting in the villa; he would surprise her. She didn't even know that he had returned, that he had been drunk for three days and three nights and had changed his ticket for an earlier flight. His temporary defeat would not upset her. She was both intelligent and active. She would inspire him with unusual but sound ideas. Lovely Viola, Charlie's private saint. Holding hands, they would overcome.

Viola was doing that already, holding on to the end of her mattress.

As Viola looked over her shoulder, her almond-shaped eyes spoke the same submissive message expressed by the position of her body. Eddy answered her subservient invitation by thrusting with even less restraint. She kept on looking into his eyes while his intense penetration made her draw up her lips. Her passionate sneer grew, and she groaned with pleasure as he repeated his onslaught.

"Whore! Worthless bitch!"

Her groaning lowered an octave. Eddy growled even more insulting terms knowing that rough treatment would increase her lust. He paused when he felt that she had reached her pinnacle and watched the shudders that coursed through her haunches. When the spasms ceased, he started again at a leisurely rhythm, more suitable to his own taste this time, and aimed at his private climax. Viola attempted to wriggle free but he hooked his hands around her hips and pulled her body closer until he was sated.

Well, that was it. He let himself drop backward and grinned. He was doing better each time as he learned to play more skillfully the part she expected. It had been difficult in the beginning; this emphasis on giving rather than taking took some doing, but her special qualities made the effort worthwhile and he enjoyed the rehearsals. Viola was the most beautifully shaped woman he'd ever put his hands on. He was lucky that she wasn't too right in the head and liked being chased by older men. He ought to be grateful.

She jumped off the bed and stretched. "I'm sweaty all over, I'm going to take a shower. Coming with me?" She held her pose for another two seconds and he admired her breasts, which she herself had once compared to juicy but firm winter pears, admired them obediently for he wasn't so interested right now.

"Later."

"Would you like me to bring you a drink?"

"If you please."

She was back within a minute and he reached longingly for the gin and lemonade, decorated with a paper-thin slice of orange delicately stuck on the glass's edge.

"Now drink that like the obedient beast you are," Viola said sweetly. "It should give you the energy to have another go at me later."

"You'd like that?"

"No, but you would."

The door clicked behind her. He sat up and studied himself in the mirror at the foot of the king-sized bed. Viola was fond of mirrors; if he looked to the side he could also see himself. In the light of the antique kerosene lamp that Viola used to romanticize her sexual dramas, his reflection appeared favorable. He turned up the wick.

Well? Not too bad, considering. He opened his mouth wide. His new teeth, cleverly cemented to filed stubs, were exact counterparts of what their originals had once been. He rolled over on his back. Belly? Not too obtrusive. True, it would flop a bit if he turned sideways, but he wouldn't do that now. He raised his legs. Very trim legs. Sitting up again he examined his eyes; the chronically burst veins were hardly visible in the soft light, but the clear-blue irises reflected quite well. A good part of Eddy's movie-star persona still lingered. His charm continued to rest on established foundations. A well-kept hero of the screen, secretly slipping into middle age.

He dropped back. A dark thought had flashed through his

brain; he grabbed its tail and pulled it back. There it was, leering at him. She had called him a "beast" again; the classification began to irritate him. Did she want him to be refined? Didn't her capacity for orgasm depend on his coarseness? He would rather be politely passionate, but if he were she would have to adjust; try to play the lady and, as the lady, deny herself completion and be forced to engage in more solitary pursuits, an ice princess frozen in her land of mirrors. He opened the drawer of the night table and saw her collection of battery-powered plastic pricks. Their colors revolted him. Cosmetic pink. Slime green. Slick ebony. Day-Glo orange. Cheap Christmas ornaments, artificial Africans, carrots. Carrots . . .

He slammed the drawer shut, pushing the association away. His back suddenly itched furiously in a spot he could not reach. He shut his eyes until it passed.

Intent on blotting out the symptom of which he wouldn't, and probably couldn't, trace the cause, he forced his mind to focus on present pleasure. What a lucky find Viola had turned out to be; what a surprising joy she was after the avid and bespectacled librarians, sorted from unappetizing busloads, that he'd had to contend with for so many years. How could he ever have accepted the telltale wrinkles, the sagging lines, the pouches of aging flesh that lotions and massage could no longer mask?

Viola hadn't lost any of her attractions since he'd seen her for the first time in a Florence alley. That fairy-like apparition, completely unexpected in a street scene that he had learned to accept as no longer an exotic part of his routine, had so frozen his body that he gaped stupidly at the woman who crossed his path.

His paralysis lasted several seconds but gave way abruptly so that he had to grab hold of a lamp post to keep from falling. He knew that he had never seen a woman like Viola, that she combined everything that he not only wanted desperately but needed. The sensation was overpowering. There was no room for doubt.

Leaning drunkenly against the lamp post, Eddy adored her flowing movements, the sensual elegance of her elfin body. He saw the small raised breasts, tight in a silk blouse. He marveled at the full but finely sculptured lips, the magnetism of her gaze. His body trembled; his hands clenched, wanting to stroke her short, thick black hair.

She had stopped to examine a window display. He started toward her, but she walked briskly on. He followed, enjoying the classic whorish flicker of her skirt, slit on both sides so that he could catch glimpses of her slender, well-wrought legs. During the minute that he was close to her, doggedly trailing what had to be a hallucination, his mind was in utter disorder. Insights formed that would have unnerved him if he'd been able to observe their birth and growth.

Later, while trying to relive those moments, he tentatively concluded that he might have been on the dark side of the moon, or even beyond the boundaries of the known universe. He knew his own secret essence. Perceived why hers was its complement. He compared her to the Delvaux paintings that attracted him so much but immediately lost interest in the exercise. She was not a model for but the source of a true artist's vision. He had known then, he told himself later, that the Earth was a planet of great power, mysteriously circling an inexhaustible supply of energy in an infinite expanse, and not a dim backdrop against which mankind performs its idiotic antics.

But these images came to him later. At the actual moment he was running after her, the spark released at the base of his spine exploded near the top of his skull, and the blast left no room for reflection.

The woman was far ahead. He saw her cross a main thoroughfare.

Car brakes pressed in panic made tires squeal as Eddy lunged into the traffic, deaf to the chorus of oaths thrown at him by linguistic artists through hastily wound down windows.

She stepped into an aging Jaguar. Even in his extreme state of bliss Eddy noticed the expensive make of the car but did not take account of the information. It mattered more that he was out of breath and unable to talk clearly. He panted and rubbed his aching side. The Jaguar was slipping away when he tapped on her window. She braked, the glass hummed down.

"Yes?"

"I must talk to you."

"Oh? Why?"

He spoke English, perhaps because of the car's make. "My name is . . . Eddy Sachs . . . got to talk to you . . . have coffee with you . . . please?"

She looked at his stuttering face. "I don't even know you."

"Never mind . . . I just saw you . . . please." He struggled to think of a smoother approach, of proper allusions to provide her with a sensible reason to get out of her car and accept his company. There was no time. She thought that he was after her, and he was, but perhaps he could make her feel safe.

"I'm Dutch, not Italian . . . it's all right . . . we can go and have coffee together." He pointed at a nearby café. She would be secure there, protected by decent-looking people and within reach of her car.

He almost fell when the Jaguar suddenly reversed, back into the parking place it had been about to leave. He tottered to her door, opened it, and supported her elbow while she got out.

"I'm Dutch too," she said. "Now isn't that a coincidence?"

"Indeed." He didn't quite believe her, how could she originate in his own prosaic homeland? But she spoke the language, faintly accented, perhaps she had lived in Italy for some years.

She accepted his arm. He guided her across the street.

She laughed. "But this is ridiculous. Why should I drink coffee with you? And what's so urgent? I really don't know you. Have we met somewhere before?"

"No, I saw you for the first time in that alley over there. You were windowshopping."

"I don't even want coffee, I just had two espressos. If I drink another drop I'll be sitting up all night."

His fears evaporated as they entered the café. He managed to evoke the dazzling smile he used only on special occasions. He adjusted his step to hers so that she wouldn't feel that he was dragging her with him. Good, Eddy thought. He was glad he had dressed well even though he had the day off and did not have to impress his tourists. His hair had been cut the day before and his shoes were polished an hour ago. His expensive watch accentuated his material well-being; he had bought it in Hamburg at a discount from one of Kroll's business acquaintances.

He found a table at the rear of the terrace. "No coffee? A Pernod perhaps?"

"No, a lemonade. Don't you think I should try to keep my head cool?"

"Waiter, two lemonades."

"With ice," she hissed.

"With ice, waiter."

She adjusted her skirt thoughtfully. "Would you mind explaining yourself? I really don't care to be picked up by strangers in the street."

"I'm sorry. I didn't want to bother you but, you see, I had no choice. I simply had to meet you. I never saw a woman like you. You are almost unacceptably beautiful."

What is this, he thought as he talked, can't I come up with something better? This is just flirting, transparent flattery.

She was smiling too but her voice was still cold. "Do you *need* something from me? Perhaps you wish to convert me to some cult." She appraised his tailor-made linen suit. "You don't wish to borrow money, do you? I never carry cash."

Eddy groped for a diversion. The terrace was set off by potted magnolias, in full bloom. He noticed how delicate the shape of each flower was, how subtly the plants' little branches supported their glorious display. He would like to share his appreciation with her. He pointed. "The magnolias are splendid, don't you think?"

She glanced at the plant. "Aren't they usually in spring? I don't care for flowers. Flowers are merely pretty."

Eddy tried to recall what he had learned at the theater school.

95

He had engaged in this type of dialogue often enough, with a director behind him suggesting expressions, correcting his posture, mouthing the line into his ear.

She rummaged in her bag and brought out a pack of cigarettes. "Are you trying to make me?"

He flicked his lighter and watched her while she inhaled slowly. He was back on familiar ground now. So she would pretend to be coarse? Perhaps divinities overreact when they suddenly find themselves on the lower planes.

She added sarcasm to her attack. "You do this as a hobby? Or are you interested professionally?"

"No."

"What do you mean, no?" She waved the smoke away and brought her face closer to his. "You're probably some superpimp. Do you own one of these exclusive clubs in shuttered villas where my husband takes clients who are hard to persuade?"

"No, no," Eddy said pleasantly.

She nodded. "Yes, yes. But let it be. You're not a pimp, I don't think Italians would allow a Dutchman to join their favorite fraternity. Maybe you just like to harass women. Does it matter what type they are? I suppose you've been living here awhile too, am I right? Most Italian men bother women but they content themselves with pinching bottoms, they don't bang on car windows. An *original,* aren't you?"

"I don't normally run after women," Eddy said flatly.

She disturbed the ice in her drink with her straw. "What do you do for a living? You're not a tourist are you?"

"I'm a guide, I work for Globus Tours."

She seemed interested. "I know that company, it advertises in the *Herald Tribune.* Their trips are exclusive to the well situated, I believe. Is that the reason that you look so smart?"

Eddy looked at the magnolias for support.

She touched his sleeve lightly. "You'll have to make conversation, you can't pick me up and then just sit and stare. There are rules to this game."

Eddy made his lighter skid over the tabletop. "They keep me

busy, there's a lot of art in Italy, the tourists have to see it all."

"You're here only for a few days to do the museums?"

"I'll be leaving tomorrow."

She laughed. "So that's why you're in such a hurry. You gave me quite a fright when you suddenly popped up next to my car. I'm getting used to you now."

A come-on; Eddy found his smile again. It was true that he didn't have much time, and besides, angels have wings. She could fly away. Now or never. He lowered his hand solemnly on hers and looked into her eyes. "May I invite you to come with me to my hotel room?"

She giggled. "You haven't asked my name. I'm called Viola."

"A lovely name, it suits you."

She blew in her glass and admired the bubbles forming around her straw. "Nearly all the men I meet try to make me, but nobody has ever run after me the way you did. I noticed you in the alley, I was sure you were following me afterward, but I didn't know whether you would talk to me. The others boast or try to perform heroic deeds for me. I prefer your approach. What hotel are you staying in?"

"The Carotti."

"I've only eaten there, I hope the rooms are as good as the food."

"They are."

"Do I have time to finish my cigarette?"

"But of course."

I would like to sit here with her for a long time, Eddy thought, and then maybe go for a walk. We could look at trees. We could embrace.

She was right, he thought as they walked to the hotel. What else can we do together? It's a hot day, my room is air-conditioned. We are adults, we can dispense with the preliminaries.

She was talking to him. "I've been a tour guide too, on a bus in Amsterdam. I met my husband in the Rijksmuseum, he's an art dealer, much older than you are. He invited me to dinner, he was very polite."

She stopped before the hotel's revolving doors. "Last chance. Tell me I can save my soul if I go home now."

"That would be against my interests and inclinations." His bantering tone hurt him. This should have been Venice; they could have rented a gondola, and kissed. All this had been too simple, but did it matter?

She undressed quickly in the room. "You'll have to kiss me first."

"Of course."

He had taken his time with her, and when they had finished room service brought drinks and snacks. She sat on the bed and began a proper conversation, as unconcerned about her nakedness as she had been when she stepped out of her underwear. She told him her surname was Vrieslander. The name made no particular impression on him.

In the months that followed they kept on meeting. He would phone her every time he arrived from Hamburg, and she would come to him at the Carotti. Once he phoned her and asked if she would like to go to Florence.

"No, not this time. Why don't you see me at my home? I'd like to show you the house, especially my garden. Empoli is more romantic than Florence."

"Your husband?"

"He's in South America."

"You're not ill, are you?"

"Wouldn't you come if I were ill?"

"Of course I'd come. I'd sit next to your bed. Hold your hand. Read you erotic novels."

"That's very sweet of you, but I feel fine. Come quickly, I hope you're in top form because you'll have to deliver again. But first I want you to admire my garden."

He was almost delayed. The Japanese group he was in charge of had appointed a representative who showed him a list of written questions they wanted answered. The questions had to do with the meaning of art. Eddy passed the document to his driver, rented a small Simca, and left the city.

It was dark when he arrived. Viola was waiting for him on the lawn in front of the villa. She took him by the hand and led him to a flat round stone, luminescent in the light of the stars. The large rock was surrounded by a bed of small, silver-colored plants bordered again by tiny bushes with pointed velvet leaves and gray-green varieties of fanlike ferns. Short cedar logs had been driven into the earth and separated the round garden from the lawn.

"Wait," she whispered and swept her arm. The moon, nearly full, was rising above the trees. "You came at the right time, this is my moon garden, the moon waited for you." Her eyes gleamed. "Now you're mine until you die and I replace you by another old man. I can only use graybeards for my spells. Only old men understand my needs."

She darted away and began to dance on the moon-bathed wooden disks of the cedar stumps, swinging her arms. "Follow me, Eddy, come."

He didn't move.

"You see, you're caught. You can't leave the rock until I release you."

She circled him thrice, chanting a song; he couldn't make out the words. Then she made her way between the plants and pulled him off the stone. They walked to the house.

"You liked my moon garden? I made it myself. I did it all, I dug and brought the soil with a wheelbarrow, moved the stone, planted all the herbs. Witches can't accept help when they do their sorcery. The work nearly broke my back. I even had to cut my nails."

"You're a witch?"

She laughed. "As if you didn't know, have you forgotten how we met? I cast my spell on you then. You had no choice but to come after me."

"Seriously?" Eddy asked. "You studied books and all that? How did you know what to plant? The garden is so well laid out, are you sure you didn't have a gardener?"

"No books. It was all in my head. The plants came from a local greenhouse, but I just pointed them out, I didn't even know their names then, they were calling out to me. I let them choose their own places too. Herbs and witches are different sides of the same dark power."

Eddy looked back. The moon was shining fully on the garden; the stone gleamed; the beds of thyme and sage seemed to shimmer with ghostly strength.

He caressed her hair.

"But I'm not only a witch, I can be anything you like." She pulled his head down and whispered into his ear. "Shall I be your slave girl?"

"That would be nice."

"Good. Your noble slave girl, of course, for I must be a princess."

He followed her through a veranda, overgrown with flowering vines. "Let me see now," Viola said. "We must get this straight or we won't know what's what. You're a king. You rode into my father's country at the head of your wicked knights, burned our castle, and swiftly beheaded all my father's soldiers. I thought you would kill me too. I leapt off the tower just before the flames reached me. But you had me pulled out of the slimy moat. I almost drowned."

Eddy shivered.

"Are you cold?"

"A chill."

"Shall I go on?" She pressed her breasts against him and peered into his face, talking softly. "I was dressed in silky robes and they clung to my moist skin. You could see my body. Your lust was aroused."

Eddy held on to a post. His voice was hoarse. "And then?"

"You had me flung into a cell and kept me there for a few days, so that I would be humble when I came out. There were rats in the dungeon. A sadistic dwarf came to see me. He made me crawl at his feet, threw me bones from your table. I drank the dregs of your wine. Finally you sent for me. Tonight we meet. You will rape me cruelly, won't you?"

Eddy cleared his throat. "That goes without saying."

"But first you'll beat me and you'll be more refined than your dwarf. Did you bring your whip?"

Eddy looked lost. "No, I'm sorry, I forgot."

She sauntered ahead. "Never mind, we can use mine. Would you like a drink first?"

Charlie left his luggage on the passenger seat and parked the Ferrari in front of the steps that connected his villa with the garden. His mail was waiting on a Chippendale side table in the hall, and he flipped through the envelopes, hoping against hope that the check from Asunción had arrived. It hadn't. It was late; Viola would have gone to bed by now. He walked on to the kitchen, poured himself a glass of milk, and took it back to the garden.

From the lawn he admired the noble architecture of Villa Vrieslander. How long would he be allowed to live here? If he couldn't stay free of the bank's clutches, the house would soon be sold to the highest bidder, very likely Verleur's incognito agent. The miserable purchase sum would be credited to his account, and the bank would still be able to pursue him for whatever he still owed. Then what? Welfare in Amsterdam?

He threw the half-full glass at a rosebush. Just imagine, Charles Vrieslander, once a millionaire, holding out his hand. A pathetic little begging hand. Ever since the gold crash he'd again been conscious of his physical smallness. He had begun his career as a little shitkicker and now he was back where he started. At kindergarten he had always made himself scarce when the games were a little rough; from now on he could abstain from any sort of game. Little Charlie is not playing anymore.

Little Charlie has to beg. The truth cut painfully through his head. Beg from the Dutch Social Service, whining for tax money paid in by neat burghers, the straight ones, his decent countrymen. They would have themselves represented by an official who loomed up in his imagination like a terrible giant. Little Charlie on his knees, nose in the dirt. "Please, sir, I'm down and out, you know. Me and my woman have nothing to eat. Nowhere to sleep either. We would like some assistance, sir, and a roof over our scurvy heads."

He would be given assistance; he was a Dutchman, after all, and help was due to him. He would be provided with a drafty loft, in a shack previously occupied by recently deported Arabs or Turks. He would be a mangy guest in his own country, fed on sticky white bread, and maybe able to squeeze in a potato croquette or a can of sardines on Sundays.

He marched across the lawn, hitting an imaginary foe with short thrusts of his arms. What could he do to evade such an impossible fate? And what was that Simca doing there, parked within his boundaries? Probably the little junker belonged to one of the maids; the silly bitches were to leave their transport in the street, but as soon as he turned his back the staff just did as they pleased. He turned around, folded his hands behind his back, and absorbed the intricate beauty of his home. The stately mansion was the sublime projection of his own mind, designed according to his directions by a famous Florence architect and built by artisans who still took pride in their work. He admired the hand-hewn oak beams that carried the balconies and the upper story cantilevered on both sides. He walked about to look at the galleries that connected the house with the rear garden via paths leading to ornamental shrubs lining his pond. He followed one of them and crossed the bridge which took him to his gazebo, a structure on stilts under which swans slept.

The moon caressed the pond, and one of the swans disconnected from the shadow and floated toward the rippling light in the pond's center. Charlie sat on the railing and lit a cigarette. In this pavilion he had thought up his best plans, sucking Cuban cigars and sipping gin and lime brought by a lovely Sicilian maid who, for a reasonable consideration, was quite prepared to straddle a table corner while accommodating the master's baser desires. Did he really have to take leave of the licentious life of a gentleman dealing in art? Did he have to give way now so that some crude bounder could move into his sphere of luxury?

He returned to the villa and entered through a rear door. He climbed the staircase, moving soundlessly, his small feet almost hidden in the high pile of the carpet.

Viola was asleep. He would spend the night with her and be strengthened by her young vitality. If he could only hold on, luck would be with him again. While he rested in Viola's arms a solution would surely pop up.

He saw her kerosene light glimmering under the bedroom door. So she was still awake. His softly calling voice trembled, "Viola?"

How can anybody get that fat? Eddy thought, observing the agitated flesh pudding at the other side of the desk.

Kroll laughed on, wiping tears out of his eyes. He removed his spectacles; his cheeks, sagging well below his jaw, trembled obscenely while his puffy, pale hands flopped spastically on the desk top. His voice had become squeaky. "I haven't heard anything that funny in a long time."

Eddy leaned over and lit Kroll's cigar for him. "I'm glad somebody enjoys it, I didn't."

Kroll sucked smoke. "Do you know that I will watch even the worst movies if I hear that they contain a scene like that? That sort of stuff never fails to amuse me. It's classic. Don Juan being driven out of the house by the irate cuckold. It still happens in our age, eh? And to Eddy! Of all people."

"That'll be enough, Paul."

Kroll covered his face. His shoulders shook. He chortled through his hands.

Eddy put his feet on the little table in front of his chair. "It wasn't at all funny. I was stark naked. That stupid little squirrel was hopping around me. He even managed to find a gun. I couldn't leave until I found my socks. It was pitiful. Down all those stairs, through a long corridor, and that idiot behind me, pushing and yelling his head off."

Kroll hooted in his handkerchief.

"You're not laughing again, I hope?"

"No no, I promise. Tell me more. Why didn't you take the gun away from him? You might have been shot."

"That's why I didn't even try. A fight would have made it worse." Eddy watched Kroll's hips protruding through the open sides of his chair. "But here's something else. I knew him. Charles Vrieslander, Major Charles Vrieslander. I met him here in Hamburg, in 1946, during the time that you were in Röherstrasse jail."

"Was Vrieslander with Allied Intelligence, too?"

"No, he was visiting the villa at the Kleine Alster."

Kroll blew smoke at the ceiling. "Freiherr von Wittenberg's house?"

"Yes."

"What was he doing there?"

"Fetching a Rembrandt I'd just pierced with a beer bottle. A troublesome situation. I managed to get out of it."

Kroll, still wiping his eyes, seemed to have forgotten his mirth. "You're sure that that was the same Vrieslander?"

"Oh yes."

"Did you remind him, the other evening when he threw you out of the house?"

"Yes, but he didn't seem to care. He was not exactly in a nostalgic mood."

"What happened to the Rembrandt?"

Eddy grinned. "He took it away, saying it would go back to the Rijksmuseum. He showed me some sort of authorization. I'm sure now that he stole it. I've visited the Rijksmuseum several times since then, every time I've gone back to Amsterdam, and the painting isn't there. I thought perhaps it had been stored, but Rembrandts are always on display. No, he stole it, it would be just the sort of thing he would do. Viola has told me enough about him; he specializes in selling fakes and loot. He looks like an old con now, hardly resembles the dapper little gent I met in 1946." Eddy paused thoughtfully. "I wonder where he took the

Rembrandt. Didn't you say that he had been on a business trip to South America?"

"Yes?"

Kroll's cigar pointed at Eddy's chest. "Freiherr von Wittenberg lives in South America, in Paraguay. What was the painting's subject?"

"A biblical figure."

"Anybody in particular?"

Eddy switched on his lighter and peered at the flame. "Solomon? No. A young king on his throne. Vrieslander did mention the name at the time. Who was it again? Something with an *a* and an *o*."

"Absalom?"

"Yes, Absalom. You think the painting is in South America?"

Kroll filled a hand with pretzels from a cellophane bag on his desk and popped them into his mouth. His jaws ground monotonously. "Yes."

"It could be anywhere."

Kroll pointed at the floor. "I don't think so. Down there, in my bar, you could have seen the Freiherr von Wittenberg, about three years ago. I was introduced to him. He has always been a big shot in Hamburg, but I only knew him from a distance. He was quite old, but he still looked every inch a Wehrmacht general. Even wore clothes of a military cut, with gold buttons and dark green ribbon set into his collar. I was allowed to sit with him for a while, in between his bodyguards. The general was holding forth about his art collection."

"Did he mention Rembrandt?"

"Yes."

"*Absalom*, too?"

"No, but he said he owned a Rembrandt. I tell you, your Vrieslander fetched that painting for him from occupied territory. Didn't you say that Vrieslander visited Bogotá?"

"He did."

Kroll refilled his mouth. "Von Wittenberg lives in Asunción, maybe Vrieslander went there too. But we are well represented in Colombia, too, of course."

"We?" Eddy asked.

"We, the Nazis."

The conversation's sudden turn upset Eddy. "You're not telling me that you still belong to the party?"

"In a way," Kroll said, "and as far as I've ever belonged to it. I was never impressed by its ideology and I always thought that Hitler was a little off. But I grew up in the party; as an SS officer I was an automatic member. Whatever is left of its highest ranks still meets regularly in my bar."

"And they all live in South America?"

"Most do." Kroll got up, rolled his chair around the desk so that it stood next to Eddy's, and sat down again. "This is a conspicuous combination of events, Eddy, a bizarre meeting of circumstances. Rembrandt's *Absalom* is now on von Wittenberg's wall, a temporary and not too final position in which both yours and Vrieslander's hands played a part."

Kroll's hand weighed heavily on Eddy's thigh. Eddy tried to move his chair but its legs were stuck in the thick carpet. "The painting is heavily damaged. When Vrieslander walked away with it, it wasn't much more than a ripped rag."

"Rips can be fixed, art restorers earned fortunes after the war. I say, *Absalom,* eh?" Kroll's fingers dug into Eddy's flesh.

"Yes?"

"An interesting figure."

"You know anything about the Bible?"

Kroll laughed. "Just about anything there is to know. My father was a parson, of the old fire and brimstone variety. An unpleasant man as most parsons are, or used to be. The trade is no longer fashionable. Absalom was David's son." Kroll threw the empty cellophane bag into the waste bin and walked back to his desk to find another. "The Book of Samuel tells us that he was the most handsome man of the time, an ancient superstar with long gleaming hair. Even the soles of his feet were lovely, that fact is stated explicitly."

"What was he doing on a throne?"

"He usurped David's position. Absalom wasn't a king for long. David engaged him in battle and Absalom had to run for his life, on a mule that didn't know the way. Happened in the woods of Ephraim, north of the Jordan River. I still know it all by heart. My father always read the holy words after dinner and would question us when he had closed the book. We had to keep our hands on the table, and he would hit us with a large silver spoon if we didn't have the right answer."

"No wonder you joined the SS."

"The SS training resembled what I had to put up with at home. Father approved. He was hit by a bomb for his troubles in 1944. They had to scrape him off the street to send him to his reward."

"And Absalom?"

"He died in the forest, hanging from a branch by his beautiful long hair. The mule kept on walking."

Eddy tried to visualize the man he had seen in the painting hanging by his hair from a branch. "Biblical bullshit. Impossible. Either the branch breaks or he pulls himself up and tears free."

"The Bible said so," Kroll said, "but it makes many claims and we mustn't forget that it specializes in morality tales. Absalom was an evil man, thus he had to die miserably."

"Evil men die in featherbeds, in South American palaces."

"Don't be angry with me," Kroll said when he let Eddy out of his office. "I'm sorry I laughed at you."

On the way to his car Eddy made every effort to forget that afternoon's conversation; Kroll did the opposite. For no apparent reason the German concentrated on the information that had come his way. He did no more work that afternoon but smoked cigars and stared out of the window, humming to himself.

Eddy drove slowly down Hamburg's Holstenwall, following instructions given by Otto von Kirst on the telephone. The wide avenue is offset by a half circle of lush parks in the midst of the city. On his right, high modern buildings reflected a lush foliage which, moving lightly in the summer wind, softened the harsh lines of the steel structures. It was Sunday morning; Otto had summoned him to a restaurant on the border of the Aussen Alster lake, a large pearl of clear water, the fitting centerpiece of Germany's fully restored, most active metropolis. He parked close to the Kennedy Bridge, next to a Corvette convertible with a Berlin license plate.

Otto waved from the terrace and met Eddy on the wooden stairs leading down to the parking area. Eddy hadn't seen his friend from the Berlin years since he left the capital. Otto had aged, but his gray temples and the deep lines connecting his sharp nose with the corners of his thin mouth made him even more sinister than he had been. He still wore a cape, flowing down from his wide shoulders. Supporting himself on a polished walnut cane, Otto led Eddy to a table where a woman was waiting. "Meet Helga."

"How do you do, Helga," Eddy said obediently. She was curled up in a wicker chair and held out a hand. Eddy kissed it. Helga was in her late thirties, but she retained the trained eternal beauty of a professional model. In spite of the welcome she expressed with the smile of her full lips and the soft warmth of her large eyes, he felt that she was cold and distant, solely concerned with her own hidden thoughts.

"Sit down," Otto growled while he lowered his tall body carefully into his chair. A grimace of pain made his mouth twitch. "Helga used to be a fan of yours."

"You look just like I remember you from your movie," the woman was saying.

"Which one?" Eddy couldn't help smiling; it had been a long time since anybody reminded him of the glorious spotlights.

"The one in which you stole a fighter. You were shot down but escaped through a swamp."

"But they got me later."

"Yes," Helga purred, "a pity. They should have given you the hero's part. It was horrible to see you feel sorry for yourself in the end." She reached for her drink, the way her hand moved was elegant, but he noticed the sudden fierce grip with which her thin clawlike fingers squeezed the glass. So Dracula finally found a fitting mate, Eddy thought. He touched Otto's stick. "An accident?"

Otto tapped the calf of his right leg, the resulting sounds were metallic. "Let's say I was on an expedition to destroy unfriendly forces and miscalculated the risk. We won, but part of me had to be replaced. It was time to leave the gymnasium anyway, I prefer my other trade."

"You're here on a visit?" Eddy studied Helga while he waited for Otto's answer. She was clad in black slacks and a matching jacket. The jacket sat loosely on her shoulders so that her breasts, held by a close-fitting T-shirt, were clearly outlined. Eddy read the words printed across the shirt in flowing pink lettering, "Don't Touch."

Otto fidgeted in his chair, trying to find a more comfortable position. "No, we have settled here. I was promoted by the organization. Hamburg belonged to the competition, but there have been some changes and we're free to explore this market now."

Eddy whistled softly. "You're in charge here? Same commodity as you distributed in Berlin?"

"The same, and the best. The organization has tightened up and we have expanded. We own our own refinery so that we can manufacture the goods to our own specifications." He touched Helga's thigh. "She's in it, too, a tried and trusted member of management. We're looking for some help to form a well-respected and well-paid nucleus in this part of the country. It wasn't easy to find you until I thought of consulting the register for foreigners in City Hall. It gives your profession as a tour guide, that's just a label I assume?"

"No."

Helga's eyes focused, her lips curled disdainfully. "You're not serious. Who do you work for?"

"Globus Tours. I've been with them ever since I left Berlin."

Otto's eyebrows formed arches. "But that's over ten years ago. You've been drifting around in buses all that time?"

"We sometimes charter planes."

"So what does that make you, a flight attendant instead of a bus conductor?"

Eddy spread his hands. "It was all I could find."

Otto shook his head. "You should have let me know. I suppose you're married too and have kids."

"No."

"Alone?"

"Not quite, but she's married."

"So, you're free," Helga said pleasantly, "that's something. Otto spoke highly of you. We're authorized to ask you whether you would like to work with us."

Seagulls planed gracefully above the lake; children were chasing a large bright blue ball on the lawn; a sailboat close by went smartly through the wind. "It's a lovely day," Eddy said.

Otto's stick tapped against Eddy's shoe. "You won't be working on street level, of course. We'll employ the existing contacts. Since we won the battle, we can use what the loser bequeathed to us.

You'll have to help me bring in stock and collect payments. I need someone who can move in any circle and is completely trustworthy. But since nobody is completely trustworthy, we have a few rules, and a saying."

Eddy had been watching a young man who was leering at Helga. Helga hadn't noticed. She excused herself and got up. The young man, egged on by his friends, followed her to the rear of the terrace. Otto's stick touched Eddy's shoe again. "Yes," Eddy said, "what's the saying?"

Otto had dropped his polite mask; his dark glowing eyes held Eddy's. "In case of doubt, throw him out." His lips drew away from his teeth. "And out means all the way out."

"Just a minute," Eddy said. Helga's admirer was waiting near the door connecting the dining room and the terrace. He was grinning at his friends. He looked like a fashionable fellow, dressed in immaculately pressed dungarees, a turtleneck sweater, and wide leather belt. The belt's buckle was a silver swastika. He couldn't be older than twenty, a tough specimen with bulging muscles and a bull's neck. Helga came out of the door. The young man's hands shot up and reached for her. The text on Helga's T-shirt was no longer visible. The assailant appeared to be kneading its contents. His friends were applauding.

Eddy was too late, a young couple carrying a baby blocked his path. He had to move around chairs and tables before he could grab Helga's assailant. The young man let go of his quarry and turned quickly. His fist came up swiftly, but Eddy expertly blocked the punch. A waiter came running.

"Don't," Helga said quietly. "Escort me back to the table."

Otto was out of his chair when they returned; he held his cane lightly in both hands and stared at the young man who was ushered off the terrace by the waiters. "Let him go," Helga said; "we don't want a scene."

"But of course," Otto said. He called for the bill, paid, and borrowed the waiter's pen. He wrote a telephone number down and showed it to Eddy. "Got it?"

"I'll remember."

Otto struck a match, lit his cigarette, and burned the paper. "Don't wait too long."

Otto and Helga left; Eddy went to the restroom. When he left the restaurant the Corvette was no longer in the parking lot. He saw the sleek car driving ahead of him as he followed the lake's shoreline on his way back to his apartment. Otto drove slowly and pointed a lone pedestrian out to Helga. Eddy recognized the young man from the restaurant jogging on the sidewalk. Otto parked; Eddy stopped too, a hundred feet behind the Corvette; he could hear Otto's exhaust gurgle. The jogger wasn't aware of the sports car waiting quietly; he passed several couples and small children and came out in the open. The Corvette jumped, climbed the sidewalk, and roared after its prey. The jogger looked around and darted off, running on the meticulously mown grass strip separating the sidewalk from the water. The Corvette swerved viciously and accelerated.

The young man was more athletic than Eddy had given him credit for. His sprint was fast, but not fast enough. He took his only safe option, the water, but the Corvette's bumper was too close. Eddy, who had edged forward, heard the impact before the body splashed into the lake. Eddy reversed, giving the Corvette room to cross the sidewalk and get back to the road. He raised his hand an inch from the steering wheel to acknowledge the triumphant smiles of the sports car's occupants. He watched the Corvette swing through the traffic ahead and lose itself in the distance.

"Where are we now?" Eddy asked.

The smartly uniformed bus driver smiled hazily. "Not sure that I know, beautiful countryside though, don't you think?"

The big touring bus had been cruising through a dreary and unfamiliar landscape for a while. "Diamond mines, perhaps," the driver said helpfully, sweeping both arms in a gesture that embraced mountains of rubble sticking up on both sides of the badly paved road.

Eddy leaned over. "What the hell is the matter with you? You sound like your mouth is bone dry."

"I'm stoned," the driver said happily.

"You're *what*?"

The driver held up a large paper bag. "Cookies. My wife baked some for me to take on the way, and I made my own, stuffed with hashish, for the holiday coming up. Must have got the bags mixed up."

Eddy sat back. A small hand tapped his shoulder. He looked round. "Yes, professor?"

The old Japanese gentleman held up a brochure. "It's eleven o'clock."

Eddy checked his watch. "So it is."

"Coffee time, coffee and cake, your program says so, right

here." The professor stabbed an accusing finger at the small print. "Here."

"Yes, professor, why don't you go back to your seat? We'll stop in a minute."

Eddy sighed as he adjusted his rear mirror and surveyed his passengers. He'd been given an assorted load this time even though everybody was Japanese. The professor headed about half of the passengers, ancient men who still wore frock coats and striped trousers, the official garb in which their country had once surrendered to the Americans. The other half consisted of equal parts of Buddhist priests, rotund men in yellow or black robes who were forever drying their sweating skulls with large handkerchiefs, and bespectacled middle-aged women, members of a Tokyo art club. The trip had begun badly, with an engine breakdown; later they'd been stopped and fined for speeding on a secondary road; now they were lost.

"Let's see the map," Eddy said to the driver. "We've got to be somewhere."

The driver grinned. "All I can tell you is that we're still in Germany."

There were potholes and the bus seemed to hit every one of them. More artificial hills showed up, industrial buildings moved by slowly.

"Find a café."

"There aren't any." The driver began to hum to himself.

"You ate a lot of those?" Eddy asked, forcing himself to keep his voice down.

"Just one, they're strong."

The dry light hand was back on Eddy's shoulder. "Coffee and cake time." The professor waved the leaflet in front of Eddy's eyes.

"Yes, sir, we're almost there."

The bus wheels whooshed in mud pools, the road narrowed, branches rattled on the roof.

Cake, cookies, why not? Eddy grabbed the microphone. "Ladies and gentlemen, I'm sorry but we are delayed a little. We should reach a suitable restaurant in just a few minutes, but meanwhile I'll distribute some home-baked cookies."

"Better have one yourself," the driver said when Eddy got back to his seat. "This road doesn't go anywhere."

After a while they came to a gate marking the end of the road. The driver stopped to read the sign. "Gravel Works. I better turn back."

The professor materialized at Eddy's side again, pointing at the door. "Please open."

The driver flicked a switch; the passengers trooped out.

"Now what?" Eddy asked.

"They'll come back."

"Can you still drive?" Eddy asked.

The driver giggled. "No, but I can fly, this thing was handling like a spaceship for the last few miles, did you notice?"

A jeep approached, manned by workers in steel hats. The man at the wheel looked up at Eddy. "Get those people out of here, this is private property."

"Sure."

Eddy thoughtlessly took a cookie out of the bag that the driver held up. He was munching another when he walked through the gate. The Japanese had spread out over the vast yard of the gravel pit and were stumbling into the way of large tracked vehicles rumbling about. One of the Buddhist priests was intoning a solemn chant and stepped daintily to and fro, lifting his skirted legs as high as they would go. The ladies held on to each other while they listened to another priest who was babbling ecstatically. The professor tried to lead his colleagues up a hill but kept slipping down on wet pebbles to gales of laughter.

"Who needs this?" Eddy asked the driver, who was rummaging about on his knees, his hands buried in mud.

"Look," the driver said. "Jewels."

"Get away." Eddy knocked the glistening gravel out of the man's hands. The drug worked on him too but he wasn't bothered by visions; what he saw wasn't a fairy tale but stark reality, indisputable truths popping up in the harsh light of his mind.

Eddy tried to wrench his thoughts free and watched the priests who had joined their preaching colleague and were bouncing around; the women and the professors surrounded the holy men and began a slow dance, going around and around.

"That's all I have been doing," Eddy mumbled, "moving in a circle, caught in the repetition of my own stupidity. I should move on again."

He walked back to the bus; the jeep caught up with him.

"I know, I know," Eddy said to the furious driver. "But what can I do? They're out of control. There's something wrong with the bus too."

"I'll call the police," the man shouted.

"Not a bad idea."

Eddy walked on; a car stopped for him and took him to a town. Eddy found the railway station. He caught the next train to Hamburg.

"What are you doing here?" the Globus Tours manager asked when Eddy walked in. "Your driver phoned last night, he said you got lost."

Eddy nodded. "I was, I'm found now. I came to say good-bye."

He spent the evening in the small bedroom of his apartment, smoking and contemplating cracks in the ceiling. He could only come to one conclusion. The drug had released him and now pointed the way.

He dialed.

"Yes?"

"Eddy here."

"We were hoping you'd call," Otto's low voice replied. "You can start tomorrow."

PART IV

It was a quarter to four in the morning and the patrol car was waiting for the light to change. The two police officers stared ahead, dreamily contemplating the neutral colors of a hollow boulevard. Vague desires were taking shape in their brains. The one at the wheel visualized vending machines; he could eat some hot sausage perhaps. His partner considered lighting a cigarette.

Eddy wasn't paying attention. Traffic lights in the early morning don't mean much; the streets they control are supposed to be empty. His speeding Datsun had ignored several sets of lights already. There were shreds of fog about, and maybe he shouldn't have driven so fast, but he'd been partying for the last few nights and there was only this little delivery job to take care of. After that he would go home. Everything had been easy for more than six months, and his awareness was low. The police car had no business being in his way, but there it was, stopped stupidly in the middle of the road. Eddy braked with so much force that his small car skidded, hitting the patrol car's rear bumper with its side. The two officers were knocked forward, like puppets hit by a furious child; their heads banged against the windshield, their view limited to the lining of their caps.

Eddy stared as the unpleasant truth of the situation became apparent. There was the white and black striped vehicle, complete with its formidable array of colored lights fixed to the roof, pushed onto the sidewalk. Inside were the two policemen, hanging in their safety belts, heads stuck to the windshield. Here was Helga's Datsun two-seater, thrown back by the collision, with its headlights crazily illuminating a window display of female mannikins showing off black lace underwear.

His predicament contained all the elements of mathematical equations remembered from high school. He saw what was given and what to be proved and was working out the required solution.

The given facts blinked up first in his brain. He could easily assume that the patrol car had only sustained light damage and would still be in excellent running order, so that the police, reduced to automatons switched to zero, would reactivate themselves in a moment and storm the Datsun. It was also given that the indignant officers would not limit themselves to charging him with driving to endanger and causing damages but would smell his breath, have him tested for drunkenness, and search the Datsun. The car contained a kilo of heroin packed in plastic, not well hidden. He knew that he shouldn't be using the Datsun for transporting contraband — the organization owned another car for that purpose, with a registration that couldn't be traced to any of its members. That car was being repaired, however, and Eddy's own car had battery trouble. Helga was on holiday with Otto somewhere in France.

The situation was bad, but perhaps not hopeless. The impulses within his skull flashed even faster. If he allowed the constables to get hold of him, he would be taken straight to the Untersuch-Gefängnis next to the Botanic Garden and beaten for as long as it took to shatter his lies. He would probably give the game away and be taken to another jail for the duration of his life. That possibility was unacceptable.

Escape was acceptable, but was it possible? Yes, because the officers were momentarily stunned and *he* was fully conscious. Did his car still work? He twisted the key. It did.

The Datsun's hood pointed at free space. Eddy drove around the patrol car and accelerated. He turned into a side street, then another, hoping to find an inconspicuous parking place. The officers didn't know what his car looked like; they would only see another stationary vehicle, lights and engine off, while Eddy crouched on the floor.

His luck was not that good. The patrol car's siren was howling already and blue flashes lit up in his rear mirror. He put his foot down further. The Datsun was new and supposedly fast; there was no reason to disbelieve the top figure on its tiny speedometer. He kept taking corners, tires squealing while he twisted the wheel. When he realized that the pursuit was too noisy and other police cars might hear and join the chase, he saw a sign pointing to a speedway out of the city.

He cursed himself while racing off in the indicated direction. Why had he ignored the organization's clear instructions? What was wrong with imitating German efficiency? This would never have happened to Otto. Otto wouldn't be foolishly racing out of Hamburg at a hundred and some kilometers an hour pursued by yapping hellhounds.

Fog enveloped both cars for a minute; Eddy concentrated on the yellow lines containing the road. Was this really so bad? He remembered the Fokker airplane taking off in similar fog. He'd felt good during its shaky flight aimed at liberty. A plane is a better escape gadget than a car. King Absalom fleeing on a mule? Eddy pushed the unwelcome image away. No need to be negative now. Absalom had David's army after him; all *he* had to deal with were two Hamburg cops. Absalom was foolish enough to get stuck in a tree, dangling by his hair. The idiot had probably been unarmed too. Eddy felt his crotch.

He had the gun, but the patrol car was gaining. A side road opened up in the woods bordering the highway. The Datsun's tires bit into a tight curve. The country road twisted along, but one corner was sharper than he estimated and the light car skimmed onto the shoulder and then further until it was straddling a narrow ditch; waving weeds shone brightly in his bouncing lights. Eddy screwed the wheel to the left again and again but the car stuck in the loose ground until a front tire finally grabbed hold of the tarmac. The car spun out of control and heeled over. Metal screeched, then crunched to a stop. Eddy's door flung open; he twisted free of the wreck and was running for the woods when the cruiser showed up, its siren howling plaintively in the still night.

"*Halt.*"

The cops were out of their car; Eddy unzipped his fly behind an alderbush.

Shots rang out. Eddy ducked to avoid the patrolmen's flashlights pricking at the undergrowth that shielded him. They were firing at the sky.

Eddy felt his leg; it wasn't too badly bruised. The blood dribbling down his cheek came from a scratch on his forehead. He was still in fine shape, and the cops didn't know he was armed; they were being as careless as he'd been earlier on. The law was mistaking him for a common drunk; circumstances were with him again. He pushed leaves aside and peered at the Datsun. A pool of gasoline was forming around the wreck. He wished the car would catch fire and destroy the heroin. He patted his pockets. No matches. His lighter wouldn't be of any use, and the cops were in the way as well.

"Come out of there, we have you covered."

Eddy grinned.

"Switch off the siren," the other officer yelled. "I'll go in there, he's probably hurt, I'll listen for him."

There wasn't much time. The cops would be radioing for assistance, getting dogs, and staging a search. Eddy moved into the road as soon as he heard the policeman crashing about close to him. The other cop was just leaving the car. Eddy steadied his gun with both hands, aiming for the man's legs. The small revolver's pop was innocent enough but the man shrieked and fell, clutching his thigh. Eddy ran past him and slid into the car.

More shots rang out from the trees as the cruiser zigzagged away and picked up speed.

Eddy parked several blocks from his apartment and walked home. He showered and changed. He kept hearing Otto's whispered warning. *When in doubt throw him out.* Eddy hadn't even left any room for doubt; he had failed completely and compromised his superiors. Helga would deny knowing anything about the heroin, but the detectives weren't likely to accept her ignorance. The resulting trouble was sure to displease Otto. The organization's deadly feelers would be out, searching relentlessly.

Otto and Helga were due back within the next few days; there was still room to maneuver. Eddy tried to remember how much he had left in his bank account; it couldn't be much since he'd been spending heavily lately. He was too tired to think much further and set his alarm before stretching out on the bed.

Kroll sat down, pressing his buttocks with difficulty in between the armrests of the iron café chair. "So there you are again, I thought you had forgotten me."

"Never." Eddy looked up from his newspaper. "Glad to see you. I would have come to your office but it's a nice day, you can use the exercise." He passed the paper. "Read that, a cop got himself shot."

"I read it. Just a fleshwound, wasn't it?" Kroll's mouth hardened as he settled further in the chair. "Why be concerned, there are cops galore. Probably some anarchist provoking the law again. He should learn to do a good job."

Eddy took the paper back and glanced through the article. "You're right, only a fleshwound. Good."

"Bad." Kroll waved a waiter down. "Beer, a liter glass, I don't like thimbles." He turned back to Eddy. "I took the trouble to call on you last month, seeing you're so elusive these days. The place was empty."

"I moved."

"You did indeed. Might have left an address. The neighbors hold mail for you." Kroll's finger prodded Eddy's newspaper. "Don't read now. Why don't you want your mail? I think it came from Holland."

"Probably tax forms."

"Don't you have relatives?"

Eddy reluctantly folded the paper. "No. I only have a sister and she moved to Canada years ago."

"Aren't you in contact with her?"

Eddy massaged his leg, he could feel the veins throbbing under the bruise. "Yes, I met her in Amsterdam last year, but she reverted to type, a burgher woman, married to some company man. I don't think I made a good impression. She said I looked degenerate and ..."

"And what?"

"I thought I shouldn't remind her of my existence anymore."

Kroll drained his glass in one continuous swallow. He smiled slyly. "I have a surprise for you. Come with me."

They drove to the villa at the Kleine Alster.

Eddy glanced at the building. "That was a long time ago."

"The past has the pleasant habit of slipping into the future via the present. This house may still mean something to you. Look, it has a new sign."

Eddy nodded. "Sex Club Sachs, is that the surprise?"

Kroll's grin seeped through his many chins. "A familiar name, as you'll have to agree."

Eddy lowered his window. It annoyed him that the words on the neatly painted and varnished sign remained the same. Sex Club Sachs. Was this a bad joke? Did Kroll have the sign put up for some specific reason? Or was this another fateful manipulation the weary traveler cannot avoid? What significance could his own name have against the silhouette of this well-kept mansion surrounded by manicured lawns? Could the association mean anything else but a sarcastic reminder of a series of jolly episodes that he would never be able to match again?

"Sachs." Kroll bubbled with pleasure.

Eddy coughed. The familiar sound brought him back to a more trustworthy reality than the fantasy the sign seemed to suggest. "Sachs is not an uncommon name in Germany."

The Mercedes slipped away from the sidewalk. "Yes," Kroll said, "you may be right but this is an extraordinary coincidence, and only one among many. When you told me about that Rembrandt, I thought I might have a look at the villa where it was stolen from, and when I discovered that it had become a brothel, I went in to investigate further." His elbow dug into Eddy's side.

"So you had a good time?" Eddy asked politely.

"Very, especially when the present owner came out for a chat. Sturmbahnführer Sachs."

"Did you know him?"

Kroll didn't hear, his hands caressed the leather-upholstered wheel.

"An ex-comrade in arms?"

Kroll's expression became even dreamier. "At the end of the war we had thirty-five divisions. Just imagine, thirty-five SS divisions, enough to win any possible battle, and what did we do? We lost because a half-witted corporal and his court of miserable sycophants . . ."

"Yes," Eddy said, "and what did your battle brother have to say for himself?"

"He had something to tell."

"Ah."

Kroll leered significantly. "About the Rembrandt."

"Ah."

Kroll raised his voice. "Von Wittenberg has the Rembrandt again."

Eddy laughed. "But we knew that, didn't we?"

"We knew nothing, we suspected something. Now we can be sure, and we also know that a certain von Kai, a Wehrmacht officer on von Wittenberg's staff, obtained it from Vrieslander and had it restored."

Eddy looked out of the window. "Is that important? Of course the painting had to be restored, it was in bad shape when I last saw it."

Kroll groaned impatiently. "There is something very interesting connected with that Rembrandt. Very interesting. I found out that the restorer, a man by the name of Lerche, lives near Frankfurt. I also followed up on what you told me."

Eddy looked surprised. "What did I give you except negatives?"

"Negatives count too, they show connections as well as positives do. That Rembrandt never hung in the Rijksmuseum. I went to Amsterdam and pretended to be a publisher working on a book on seventeenth-century art. One of the museum's curators remembered that Rembrandt's *Absalom* was auctioned during the thirties and purchased by the art collector Eliazar de Mattos."

"A Jew?"

"Certainly. The curator even knew that von Wittenberg obtained the Rembrandt when his staff raided the Jew's house and that the Rembrandt has not been seen in Holland since."

Eddy no longer slouched in his seat.

Kroll's fist banged the wheel. "We have to have a go at Lerche. That man is an expert, a painting worth millions is not repaired by an amateur. He can lead us on. Lerche is still alive, so is von Wittenberg, so is Vrieslander. The trail is fresh, although it started long ago. De Mattos is dead of course, his ashes are in Poland."

"Go on, or is that all?"

"If it were, it wouldn't be enough. Von Wittenberg was a regular Army general, not a Nazi, but he followed Goering's rule. The conquered countries had to be stripped of all treasure. The Freiherr was clever enough to pounce before the Nazis had coordinated their looting. Dutch art treasures were destined for the SS, the center of our power, its brain and true courage. Von Wittenberg knew that we would rake the wealth together systematically, but we weren't ready yet when he met the picture framer Vrieslander in 1941."

The Mercedes turned and Eddy looked at the spires of Hamburg's restored St. Jacob's Church, neatly divided by Kroll's raised hand. "The picture framer Vrieslander," Kroll said, "was your Vrieslander's father and known as German-friendly, an official term in those days as you will recall. When von Wittenberg set out on his quest, he collaborated with father and son Vrieslander. Are you following me so far?"

Eddy was listening passively. "How come you know that much?"

"I hired a private detective in Amsterdam and asked him to check on Vrieslander. I didn't mention von Wittenberg, the sleuth came up with it."

Eddy shrugged. "You're not telling me that you intend to go to Paraguay to pick up the painting, are you? It would be easier to steal a Rembrandt from the local museum, that way you won't risk being bitten by the Doberman of a retired general."

Kroll forced the car slowly through a group of schoolboys who were standing in the road holding on to their bicycles. He ignored their protests. "You're on the wrong track. Von Wittenberg ordered his men, under the command of von Kai, to raid the homes of Jewish art collectors in Amsterdam, following a list provided by the Vrieslanders."

"Good old Charlie."

"Plural, your friend is called after his father, but never mind them now. Sachs of Sex Club Sachs knew von Kai. Von Kai was arrested in 1945 by one of your clever colleagues working out of the villa at the Kleine Alster and was shot when he tried to escape, with one of von Wittenberg's other lackeys, an officer by the name of Erbhaber. Erbhaber was dead when they carried him back to jail, but von Kai still had something to say, on a most interesting subject. You guess what it was."

"No," Eddy said, "I've always been bad at guessing."

"Von Kai was mumbling about a painting by Rembrandt, a portrait of King Absalom."

Eddy put up his hands in despair. "Which, as we know, landed up in Paraguay."

"And has two sides."

"What?"

Kroll laughed. "A painting has two sides, right? A front and a back. So von Kai said, while he was vomiting blood and on his way out forever."

The conversation continued in a restaurant where Kroll ate an entire salmon, working quietly from the tail to the head.

"Listen, Eddy," Kroll said without interrupting his feast, "I don't believe in haphazard events, no intelligent man does. In whatever happens around us definite connecting lines can be drawn. That you of all people had to pick Vrieslander's wife as a mistress must be an important factor in what we've got ourselves into now. I agree that I'm using my intuition, an inexact tool, but so far it has never failed me. When you interrogated me in the Röherstrasse cell, I knew you would release me. I also knew I would be successful in business and able to repay my debt to you. In some way or other the villa at the Kleine Alster, the Rembrandt, Vrieslander — I don't know the man and I have no idea what the painting looks like — are links in a chain that has yet to end. I would suggest that we follow the chain, up to the point where we can pull it."

Eddy picked up the wine bottle and placed it in such a way that the dead eyes of the salmon no longer looked at him. "Are we going to Frankfurt then?"

Kroll pulled the dish toward him. The fish's eyes again stared at Eddy. "Yes, if we leave now we can still make it today." He pricked one of the salmon's eyes on his fork, inserted it carefully between his teeth, and closed his eyes while it cracked. He only opened them again when he had swallowed. "Are you with me?" His fork aimed at the other eye.

The eyeless fish head made Eddy think of Otto's malevolent features. The Corvette could be snarling into Hamburg right now. He had only met with Kroll to ask for a loan, but this lead might be pointing at a fresh horizon. A trip to Frankfurt should set him on his way again. He clicked his heels under the table and bowed his head while he smiled.

"Move along please," the loudspeaker attached to a police Porsche's roof said. "Move along."

Kroll waddled back to his Mercedes. "May as well go. Why don't you drive the rest of the way?"

Police in white leather coats and orange helmets were herding people back to their cars. "Yes," Eddy said, still watching the fearful scene. A large truck had pushed two compacts off the road and was now leaning over them, crushing them slowly. He saw the truck's driver, who had climbed out of the side window of his cabin, stagger about helplessly.

The Mercedes drove off, picking up speed rapidly. Kroll fumbled with a cigar. Eddy pushed the dashboard lighter. "The fellow must have been overly tired."

"Nodded off." Kroll puffed placidly on his cigar.

"The people in those little cars will be dead by now, I saw blood trickling through the cracks. Could you hear them scream?"

"I certainly could."

"Poor bastard," Eddy said.

"Who?"

Eddy's right shoulder raised slightly. "The truck driver, of course, once his state of shock subsides he'll feel guilty."

Kroll's meaty lips thinned out in the corners. "Guilt, bah. It's a typical German feeling these days. My nephew suffers from it, he's under therapy, his parents are having a hard time paying for the treatment. The psychiatrist claims that the little sucker suffers from a war syndrome, but the boy was born twenty years after it was all over. Just imagine. That's true lunacy."

Eddy kept quiet.

Kroll intertwined his fingers on his belly. "True madness. Everything just happens, but we always insist on feeling responsible even when we weren't around when it happened. Got to explain our actions, prattle about duty to society, there's no end to the labels we will stick on neutral deeds. In reality we just do what seems profitable at the moment."

"We take the easy way out?"

Kroll patted Eddy's knee. "Right."

"And that's good?"

"No. Not bad either. It's just human behavior. As soon as you call it something you create unnecessary morals. That's what the holy books do, the Bible for instance."

Eddy looked at his watch and moved up the cruise control of the car. "That accident delayed us by half an hour. The Bible? Didn't you tell me that you know the book by heart? You wasted your time then, learning all that stuff."

Kroll grinned. "Not altogether, sometimes you have to study something before you can put it away. It helped me form my own opinions."

"Let's hear some."

Kroll wiped cigar ash from his paunch. "I'll illustrate. Remember Absalom?"

Eddy grinned. "Would I forget the golden king?"

"This is about his sister. Girl by the name of Tamar who managed to get herself raped by her half-brother Amnon. All three of them had the same father, David, but Absalom and Tamar had a different mother. Tamar is a lovely name, and the girl herself was lovely. Can you see her? One of these sensuous Jewish superbitches with the eyes of a doe, inviting trouble? She got it and Absalom felt that it was his task to set things straight again. A taboo was broken and somebody had to do something, somebody being Absalom, an interested party. If he does nothing he can't sleep well; seems like a clear argument, everybody believes it. But what really went on?"

"Tell me," Eddy said. "You're the Bible expert."

"Absalom was jealous. When I was little I also wanted to possess my beautiful sister, and if my brother had grabbed her — and he did, I'm sure, because he was the oldest and my sister thought he was wonderful — and she had come to me afterward, crying and pointing the finger, I would have gotten him, provided of course there was an opportunity. There wasn't because there were police about, slithering in the rain on their silent bicycles."

Eddy laughed. "It rained a lot in those days did it?"

"In my memory, sure." Kroll scowled. "I grew up in a nasty climate. Father's thunder and lightning in the house, and the cops outside, they always arrived unexpectedly whenever we had something good going. An ordered society. It must have been easier during the Old Testament days; a rural population, what laws there were weren't enforced, man could still do as he liked. It wasn't necessary yet to behave."

The car rode easily; Eddy's eyes were half closed. "Later man did?"

"Of course he did, then he did as he was told."

Eddy straightened up. "I seem to recall there were some atrocities."

"During the war there were." Kroll waved his cigar. "But doesn't what happened prove my hypothesis? Hitler removed the rules, and thereby all guilt."

"Didn't he go too far?"

Kroll had cheered up again. "Yes, and you're in the wrong lane, move over or we'll miss the turnoff."

"So some rules do apply?"

Kroll turned to Eddy, groaning at the effort. "There are practical rules, but they have nothing to do with morals. Hitler made us kill unnecessarily, that's where he went wrong."

They sat in silence for a while, aware only of the hum of the car and their own thoughts.

Eddy lit a cigarette. "I still don't quite see what Lerche is going to do for us."

"Lead us on."

"To where?"

"Absalom is still the clue."

"How did Absalom die? From exposure? He just hung there forever?"

"No. Turn at the next sign, we're almost there. Lerche lives in a town called Three Oak."

"How did he die?"

"He was stabbed," Kroll said impatiently. "By General Joab, a friend."

Eddy was serious now. "Quite impossible, Kroll, you must have got it wrong. Hanging by his hair, waiting to be stabbed. Absalom could have torn himself free, fought somehow."

"Stabbed by Joab," Kroll said stubbornly, "because Joab thought David would reward him."

"Was Joab rewarded?"

"No, he was made to feel guilty."

"Like your nephew?"

"Stop the car," Kroll said, "we must be close. I'll ask that man over there. Sir? Josephstrasse?"

The passerby told them the way.

Eddy parked the car in front of a Hansel-and-Gretel house surrounded by a well-arranged vegetable garden.

"I hope he's home," Kroll said, sliding out of the car. "It seemed better not to make an appointment, we didn't want him to be nervous in advance, did we?"

"Why should he be nervous?"

Kroll's ample shape surged ahead. "You'll soon find out."

A bamboo birdcage hung from a rafter of the veranda where a white canary sang high, precise notes. The three men stood on the path between the garden and the house, out of view from the street behind a hedge of beanstalks attached to tall poles. The scene was rustic, Eddy thought, and so was Herr Lerche — an ancient garden-gnome dressed in a carefully patched shirt and blue work trousers held up by wide, pale red suspenders — a man smoking a pipe who, leaning on his hoe, lovingly beholds the health-giving greens while discussing the simple pleasures of country life with city folks who dropped in for a chat. An acceptable subject for a painting. But it might be improved if Kroll would put his gun away.

Eddy studied the modern, gleaming blue weapon and its barrel poking between Lerche's suspenders.

"Come along, Lerche," Kroll barked, "our car's outside."

It took awhile before Lerche reacted. His lower jaw dropped and his pipe fell to the ground. The iron blade of his hoe crunched into the gravel while he bowed submissively. "But what do you want of me? Money? Should I go get money?"

"Come along," said Kroll.

"Where are you taking me?"

Kroll's faded eyebrows shot up sardonically. "You don't want me to . . ."

Lerche faltered, unable to resist the pistol's pressure. "Please . . ." His jaw snapped back with a dry click and his unshaven chin vibrated.

The interrogation in the car took Eddy back to a gray schoolroom, and the childhood game of questions and answers that moronic teachers play to keep restless children caught between damp walls. Kroll had found the right tone of voice, the nasal arrogant mincing way of speech that temporarily powerful officials, themselves free of supervision, know how to use with authority.

"Rembrandt, that name will surely mean something to you, Lerche."

"Yes," Lerche said obligingly, "yes."

"Have you ever handled a Rembrandt?"

"Yes. Certainly."

"I'm thinking of the year 1945. Were you involved with a Rembrandt at that time?"

"Yes."

"What was the subject of that particular painting?"

"Absalom."

Kroll grunted contentedly. "Very good. I'm so pleased that you're willing to cooperate a little. Now tell me, why did Absalom's portrait come your way?"

Lerche, grinning obediently, seemed to have trouble getting enough air. "It was damaged, ripped. I had to repair it."

"On behalf of whom?"

"Of a Dutch officer."

"Name?"

Lerche coughed nervously. "I can't remember."

Kroll's pistol jerked. "Think. What was that officer's name?"

"Vries . . . Vries . . ."

Kroll smiled. "Good enough, his name was Vrieslander, we're getting somewhere. And who told Vrieslander to bring you that painting?"

Lerche's jaw muscles worked frantically under his wrinkled skin.

Kroll raised his voice. "Aren't you talking to me anymore, Herr

Lerche? You must continue your pretty song or a lovely little bullet will pop out of this neat round hole." He touched Lerche's cheek with the gun's barrel. "Then you'll never be able to sing again. Who sent Vrieslander to you?"

Lerche swallowed. "Freiherr von Wittenberg."

Kroll's free hand tried to wave his cigar smoke out of the car. "It's getting stuffy in here. Eddy, why don't you turn off into that path over there? Maybe Herr Lerche will talk easier when we have some fresh air."

Eddy steered the Mercedes into the woods, following a trail overshadowed by tall firs. The car bounced over roots and its wheels slipped on wet moss. The path narrowed and the car's chassis hit a rock. Eddy shook his head at the ominous rattle. "We can't go much further."

Kroll got out, prodding Lerche with his gun. Eddy followed.

Kroll wheezed; the exercise seemed to have exhausted him. "This is a nice spot, embraced on all sides by Mother Nature. There's no hunting at this time of the year, so nobody will disturb us. You stand over there, Lerche."

Eddy sat down on a fallen log. Kroll lowered himself carefully on a rock. Lerche stood. "Can I sit down?"

"Why?" asked Kroll. "You look more decorative standing up."

"My legs hurt."

"I'm sorry to hear that. How old are you?"

"Eighty-two." Lerche's deep-set eyes glinted proudly, as if he were trying to impress the enemy with his ability to survive both disease and disaster.

"Stay where you are," Kroll said, "so that we can observe you better. The painting belonged to Freiherr von Wittenberg, and Major Vrieslander delivered it to you. Did Vrieslander return it to the Freiherr again?"

"I suppose he did."

Kroll wiped his forehead with his handkerchief. Eddy moved about on his log, wondering whether Kroll intended to beat the old man up.

The silence seemed to bother Lerche. "The painting is now in Paraguay. If you're interested in putting your hands on it, you won't have much of a chance." A trickle of strength had crept back into his voice. "What do you want of me?"

Kroll sighed. "Do you know von Wittenberg?"

Lerche coughed up some slime and watched while the little blob of foam disappeared between fir needles. "Yes, but not well."

"Where did you two meet?"

"At the party after the great parade in Frankfurt in 1939."

"Now what on earth would you be doing there?"

Lerche suddenly smiled. "I helped arrange it."

Kroll picked up a fir cone; the glistening sap oozing from its scaly surface made it stick to his fingers and he threw it away. "Don't tell me you were a member of the party?"

Lerche straightened up. "I was. I was also a member of the party committee and the Freiherr came over and talked to me. He said he collected art and would get me some work."

Kroll contemplated Lerche's statement. "Party member, eh? You'll have changed your ideas in the meantime I'm sure."

The old man's body stiffened. "No."

Kroll jumped up. "Herr Lerche, please accept my apologies. My name is Paul Kroll, ex-Obersturmbahnführer Kroll, GrossDeutschland Division. Please sit down." He looked at his gun. The weapon's presence seemed to surprise him. He lifted his belly and stuck it back into his belt.

Lerche tottered in the direction Kroll indicated but stopped halfway. He brought the Nazi salute shakily. "*Heil* Hitler, Herr Kroll."

Kroll raised his arm briefly. "Allow me to introduce my colleague. Eddy Sachs, ex–staff officer of the Germanic SS Division of the Netherlands."

Eddy got up and put out his hand.

"*Heil*, eh . . ." Lerche said. "Good day, Herr Sachs." He shook Eddy's hand.

Kroll watched and smiled. "You're among friends, Herr Lerche.

I will be free and frank with you, as I should after the unpleasant way you were handled just now. Listen, Herr Lerche, does the name von Kai mean anything to you?"

Lerche sat down. "It does."

"Did he have something to do with the Rembrandt as well?"

"Yes, he and Lieutenant Colonel Erbhaber. They came the day after Herr Vries . . ."

"Vrieslander."

". . . Herr Vrieslander brought me the painting."

"And?"

Lerche cleared his throat but did not say anything and looked away. Kroll bowed and stretched his arms. His fingers were clawed as if he wanted to tear at the veil that protected Lerche's information.

The old man's eyes rested briefly on Eddy's face. Eddy smiled helpfully.

"The Aue and the Leda," Lerche whispered, "do those names mean anything to you?"

"Two small rivers? Between Emden and Oldenburg?"

"Yes." Lerche's bony hand plucked at the material of his trousers. "Who do you represent now, Herr Obersturmbahnführer?"

"Like you," Kroll said softly, staring into Lerche's eyes, "I never changed my loyalty. I represent the party, Herr Lerche."

Lerche nodded. "The gold is buried between the Aue and the Leda."

Kroll breathed deeply. "Dutch gold?"

Lerche shook his head. "Perhaps, the Freiherr was stationed in the Netherlands, wasn't he?"

"He was."

"Dutch gold then. All I know is that Major von Kai and Oberst Erbhaber mentioned gold. They made me reproduce their map carefully, before they themselves indicated the precise location." Lerche's voice had become firm and friendly. "That Major Vries . . . didn't even know that a map was drawn on the painting's back, he was only concerned about taking a Rembrandt to Paraguay. We wrapped it around his chest, making sure he didn't see the markings on the back side."

"Back side," whispered Kroll, "*Gott* . . . I was right. A map, just as I suspected."

"Wouldn't von Wittenberg have been informed?" Eddy asked.

Kroll slapped his thigh. "There wasn't enough time. Erbhaber and von Kai were arrested shortly afterward, then shot. Von Kai tried to tell Sturmbahnführer Sachs but he couldn't complete his message." He looked at Lerche. "You have no idea how grateful I am to you, sir."

"But surely you informed the Freiherr," Eddy said to Lerche.

The old man looked at the ground. "No. I thought the matter didn't concern me. I was only asked to draw the map. The officers were shot?"

"Yes." Kroll jumped up. "I'm glad the secret was safe with you. We will now find the gold and I can assure you it will be used well. The party lives on and is active, we are preparing the New Order."

Eddy touched Lerche's arm. "The map business is not quite clear to me. You drew lines on the reverse side of the Rembrandt?"

Lerche nodded. "Yes, but they weren't just lines. You see, Major von Kai came to see the painting and happened to notice that the two main tears were rather similar to the way the Aue and Leda appear on maps. He showed me a staff map of that area and told me to bring out the likeness even more. After that he and the Oberst drew in more details, pinpointing the place where they had buried the gold. Or so I suppose, for they asked me to leave the room while they worked."

"So anybody who doesn't know what rivers the tears represent will never be able to make any sense of the riddle."

"Exactly, Herr Sachs."

Kroll laughed uproariously. "I would never have expected Wehrmacht officers to be that clever. Aue and Leda. Very ingenious indeed."

Lerche got up and disappeared among the bushes.

"Eddy," hissed Kroll, "there is a spade in the Mercedes's trunk. Get it for me."

Eddy found the spade but put it back again. "I don't see it."

Kroll walked to the car. "Probably moved under the spare tire, a little army spade with a hinged handle." He had his pistol in his hand again but put it on the tire to draw the spade out of the trunk. Eddy picked the gun up.

Kroll stared stupidly. "What are you doing now?"

Eddy put the gun in his pocket. "There's no need to get rid of him. I'll just hold this for you."

Kroll's hands tightened on the spade's handle. "No need? Who knows what contacts Lerche still has? If the neo-Nazis hear what we got hold of, they will turn the whole world inside out to find us. Lerche knows our names and he's seen the number on my car."

"Nonsense, he won't tell anyone, he's too busy with his beans and lettuce."

Kroll banged his spade on the spare tire. "You've no idea what the treasure consists of."

Eddy shrugged. "Money."

"Gold bars." Kroll waved the spade. "Every grain of gold that the Wehrmacht could sweep up in Holland is waiting for us, neatly buried."

"I believe you, you've done well, Kroll. I think I'll go for a piss too. Now let go of that spade and close the trunk. If Lerche is reported as missing, the police will be combing the area and we'll be foul of the law before we've even started."

Eddy admired the foamy liquid that connected him to a tree trunk. "Krauts," he said to a crow flying by, "you have to watch them all the time."

The benumbed doorman of the champagne bar came alive when he noticed the unsteady gait of potential customers. He bent one knee and made his arms swing out to the door. "Step right up. Frankfurt's best bar and most willing women await you, my genial gentlemen. Truly superior ambience; naughty niggers on drums and other instruments. Nudity and forbidden pleasures."

Kroll wavered. The doorman smiled sardonically as he shoved gently.

"Come along, Eddy," Kroll croaked, "this looks good."

The headwaiter measured the doorman's catch.

"Party pigs," whispered the doorman.

"Guests of honor," shouted the headwaiter.

Women slid off barstools, waiters ran up.

Kroll surveyed the empty stage, made of colored glass, filled with flashing bulbs. "But there's nothing there."

The headwaiter bowed. "There soon will be, dear sir. Lovely Loretta and her racy show, thought up with you in mind."

"Racy? Dirty you mean, right?"

The headwaiter guffawed behind his hand.

"Dirty or not?"

"Would sir like it to be dirty?"

Kroll belched suspiciously. "What do you mean?"

"He means," Eddy said, "whatever you want him to mean."

143

A client at the next table joined the conversation. "The head-waiter is a splendid fellow."

"You are?" Kroll asked.

"I am," the headwaiter said.

"Very well then."

"Thank you, sir. Our best bubbly?"

"Right away."

"A nice cigar to go with it?"

"Bring the box."

Corks hit the ceiling; foam splashed and was wiped off the table with a damask napkin. A woman dressed like a rabbit brushed her tail against Kroll's thigh; another hostess inserted a finger between the spongy rolls of his neck. Kroll roared hoarsely and pulled them both on his knees.

Eddy shook his head at a third girl and pointed at Kroll.

The girl pouted and swayed her hips.

"He pays," Eddy said.

She pulled up a chair and tickled Kroll's ear.

A barechested black man dressed in a straw skirt broke loose on drums. The lights went out. A white beam pierced the smoky room and played on the stage. An oriental woman appeared, carrying a box which she set down in the middle of the glass floor. A throaty flute accompanied her movements as she contorted her lithe body; the drums throbbed; a vibraphone tinkled softly.

The dancer stripped while the box opened slowly. A fat green snake unrolled its gleaming coils and raised a large flat head. It slithered up the dancer's legs, stuck to her hips, and caressed her breasts.

Kroll couldn't see; the heads of the hostesses were in the way; he pushed them aside wanting to applaud, but the girls held on to his hands.

The snake flicked its forked tongue. Its head inched down again, aimed for his mistress's curly mound. The snake's tail was twisted around her neck; its tip rested against her lips.

The spotlight held the reptile's head; a deep red glow crept up out of the stage and enveloped the stripper's trembling pelvis.

The drumming gave way to dry clicking of sticks; an eery arpeggio escaped from the vibraphone; the flute held its breath.

The snake hesitated and withdrew its head, the flute fluttered briefly on a high clear note, the drums died down.

The snake attacked, but only with its tongue. It touched and pierced. The dancer breathed in sharply. Her tiny hiss of ecstasy, amplified via a microphone, drew raucous applause.

The lights came on again.

"Not bad," Kroll said.

"Truly magnificent," said his neighbor, his dignified stutter identifying him as an Englishman. He turned to Eddy. "I trust the climax pleased you?"

"It did."

The Englishman got up shakily and followed his outstretched hand. He lost his balance; Eddy caught him and escorted him back to his table.

"Thank you. What is your name?"

"Absalom."

The Englishman rose again. "Son of David." He hiccuped. "But no matter, my grandmother seems to have been Jewish too." He sat down next to his chair.

"Sir should leave now," the headwaiter said, "after sir has paid."

"Good-bye," Kroll said, watching the reeling guest being marched away.

Several pairs of arms entwined Kroll's neck affectionately. He squeezed a wrist. "Why don't you shove off?"

"Who, me?" the rabbit girl asked.

"All of you. My partner and I must talk."

"But we're having such a good time with you."

"Fuck off."

The hostesses left.

"Is everything all right?" Kroll asked.

Eddy showed his teeth. "Everything is fine."

"Come closer."

Eddy moved his chair.

"Listen here," Kroll whispered, "we're going after that Rembrandt."

"So we will."

"And photograph the back."

"Right."

Kroll drank. "And come back straight-away." Kroll wrinkled his nose. "This stuff is nothing but sweet shit. Waiter!"

"Sir?"

"Whiskey."

The strong liquor released his temper, and he began to talk loudly while the combo behind him slid easily into a romantic ballad, accompanying two attractive lesbians on swings who undressed each other as they met rhythmically in the air. His voice interfered with the act and the headwaiter hovered around, frowning and touching his lips.

Kroll bent closer to Eddy. He confided that everything that had happened to him since the war was shit. *Scheisse*. Success in business was *Scheisse* too. So was his Freier Adler. Kroll laughed scornfully. Free Eagle indeed, hadn't the bar tied him down? Like the car agency? Nothing but a miserable routine, which Kroll now had his fill of. His hands flopped about on the table, upsetting glassware. A waiter brought fresh drinks. "And I'm getting *old*."

His agonized roar made the lesbians' swings crash into each other. The flute shrieked, the drummer missed a beat.

"Your bill, sir."

"Not yet." Kroll produced a note and showed his credit cards. The headwaiter withdrew. Kroll held up his glass and winked at Eddy. "All is *Scheisse*. Your health."

Eddy took a sip. "Gold too?"

Kroll's blunt finger pressed down on Eddy's nose. "Gold too, up to a limit. A little gold is *Scheisse*. Quite a bit of gold is still *Scheisse*. A lot of gold is something different altogether."

"I see."

"You don't." Kroll burped. He took his finger off Eddy's nose. His elbow missed the table. He brought it up again and placed it

146

firmly in an ashtray. "I will explain. What I have is never enough unless I pamper it, stick to it all the time."

His hand reached out again but Eddy slapped it away.

"I'm drunk," Kroll said sadly.

"You certainly are."

Kroll closed his eyes and shook his head. "Never mind. Let me go on. A little gold needs work, management, continuous care, right?"

"Yes."

Kroll dropped his voice. "I am stuck in shit. Nowhere to go, caught, like in the Röherstrasse, but a lot of gold . . ." He flapped his arms. "Fly away, into the great beyond." He tapped Eddy's knee. "No more *Scheisse*. Total wealth equals complete freedom. The final solution, and still in time."

He pumped whiskey into his cheeks and contemplated weightlessness. The vision elated him. Kroll flapped his arms and squeaked with joy. "What is the treasure, Eddy? A key, a golden key."

The hostesses tried to stage a comeback; Kroll pushed them away.

"A key to where?"

"To heaven."

"And where might heaven be?" Eddy asked.

"In Tenerife."

Eddy, taken aback by this sudden precise location, stared while Kroll held forth. He had, he whispered, found a magnificent mansion in Tenerife, for sale at a price nobody could afford. A palace with an ocean view, surrounded by parks. "I will buy it for you."

"For me?"

"And for me. It's fully equipped." Kroll ticked the options off on his fingers. "Olympic swimming pool. Four-car garage. Stables. Sunken marble bathtubs." He held up his thumb. "And the kitchen, ah . . ."

"Does it have a refrigerator?"

Kroll, hurt by Eddy's indifference, looked about for something to do. Waiters carried a foam-filled tub from which a naked lady waved. Kroll climbed the stage and scooped bubbles out of the bath, blowing them toward the audience. He tried to stand on one leg while performing his feat but collapsed in a heap. The head-waiter helped him up and led him back.

"Let's go," Eddy said.

Kroll didn't hear and insisted on further descriptions of Val-halla. A mystic element crept into his monologue. Heaven, he claimed, only works when it can be shared. Kroll tried to embrace Eddy. "Stay with me, I'll always take care of you. And cook for you, every night." He described his favorite dishes, sputtering with enthusiasm. Tongue in caper sauce. Shrimp stew garni. Sole au Kroll.

Please, prayed Eddy silently, release me from this pig's head. I don't ever want to eat with him again. I just did, in that two-star greasy spoon for gluttons. He choked on a meatball.

Kroll talked on, his slurred words floating on spittle. Then he sneezed and a solid streak of greenish mucus shot from both nostrils, splashing the tablecloth and Eddy's drink.

Eddy left the table and ordered soda water at the bar. Kroll followed and was made to sign a credit card slip. He stabbed at it with the waiter's pen until Eddy directed his hand.

"Where's the car?"

"You left it in a parking garage," Eddy said, "it's too far to walk. Taxi!"

The cab driver studied Kroll. "I just cleaned my car, Fatso will be puking in it."

"He's all right."

The driver shook his head. The cab pulled off.

Eddy let go of Kroll; Kroll's bulk slanted dangerously over the pavement. Eddy grabbed him again. "We'll walk after all."

A long dreary street stretched ahead, dismal under cold rain. Clouds racing above high buildings showed ragged edges. A lone songbird announced daybreak from a half-bare tree.

"Come *on*," shouted Eddy.

A truck came thundering through the next intersection, crashing its many gears and coughing compressed air from its brakes. Kroll fought free from Eddy's grip and tottered on the edge of the sidewalk, his hundreds of kilos out of balance and leaning toward the street. Eddy reached out, but his mind wasn't clear and he pushed instead of pulled. Kroll heeled over; his head slammed into the side of the truck. The enormous vehicle rattled on. There seemed to be no end to its corrugated flank.

The collision had pushed Kroll over on his back. Kroll no longer had a face.

Eddy sat on his haunches. I'm short of cash, Eddy thought. I also have to leave the country.

He looked about him; the street was empty again.

Eddy ran around the corner, Kroll's wallet and car keys in his pocket.

My only choice, Eddy thought as he drove the Mercedes out of the garage.

He didn't think again until he awoke twelve hours later in a cheap motel and opened the curtains. Sunlight flooded the room, reminding him of the gold buried safely between the magic rivers. He smiled while he shaved.

PART V

"Eddy who?" Viola asked.

"I'm on my way to see you."

"What on earth for?"

Eddy kicked the glass door. "Don't be like that, darling, I'm in a telephone booth and almost out of coins."

"Where?"

"In Florence. Is your husband with you?"

"He's in Rome, he said he'd be back tomorrow."

"Good, I have to see him too . . . Are you still there?" Eddy asked.

"Where else would I be? Do you know it's been three months? And what's this with Charlie?"

A taped voice interrupted. "You have one more minute."

"I was working," Eddy said, "and I did write to you but you never answered."

"Did you expect me to?"

Eddy hung up.

*

Villa Vrieslander's lawn was badly in need of mowing. The ornamental lanterns flanking the driveway didn't burn. Packing cases were stacked outside the garage. Viola came to the car, dressed

153

in jeans and a jersey, holding a small spade. She averted her face when he embraced her.

"Hello," Eddy said into her hair.

"Looking for a free fuck?"

He mumbled endearments. She hissed at him, "What the hell do you think I am? One lousy postcard in three months. You think I would wait for you? Get out of here."

He looked at the house. "What happened, are you moving?"

"Yes."

"So why are you working in your garden in the middle of the night?"

"It's a moon garden, remember?" Viola asked. "I was digging up its power, it'll have to go with me."

He leaned against the car and put his hands in the side pockets of his jacket. She stamped her foot. "Stop that."

"Stop what?"

"Looking so obnoxious and adorable." She tried to stab him with her spade. Its blade hit the car's window as he swung her off her feet.

*

Charlie stood in the open doorway and observed the sleeping couple. "Good morning, I hope I'm not disturbing you."

"Back already?" Viola asked sleepily.

Charlie's chin pointed at Eddy. "Same bastard, or another with the same color hair?"

"Same bastard, dear, and please go downstairs so that we can get dressed. You're not going to make a scene I hope."

Charlie stepped back and closed the door. Eddy turned over on his side. His groping hand found the gun that he had put on the floor under his jacket. Viola stroked his arm. "You won't need that just yet, Charlie doesn't get as excited as he used to. I think he went to his pavilion, why don't you visit him there in a little while? It's better that the proposition comes from you, he's likely to lose his temper when I tell him what to do."

"Can I have a shower first?"

"You can have anything you like. We really need Charlie, do we?"

Eddy answered from the bathroom, his face covered with shaving cream. "Yes, he knows the Freiherr and the Freiherr has the Rembrandt."

"Can't we go without Charlie and say that we're art historians and just want to have a look at the painting?"

Eddy's razor scraped a clean swath on his cheek. "We could, but the Freiherr might not be impressed. Don't forget that the painting is stolen and the legal heirs of Eliazar de Mattos may still be looking for it."

"But isn't von Wittenberg quite safe in Paraguay? Why would he be scared of us? Can't I seduce him?"

Eddy grunted into his towel.

"I'm quite pretty, you know." She pirouetted around him. "Old gentlemen go positively nuts about me."

"Von Wittenberg isn't old, he's ancient. I imagine he's beyond all that. No, I believe that it would be better if we were introduced properly, by somebody he trusts."

"Like Charlie?" She laughed.

"Like Charlie."

She sat down on the edge of the bathtub. "Turn around, will you?" She slapped his buttocks. "Don't gays ever bother you?"

"Not lately."

"But women do?"

"Just a little, and only if I keep my stomach in."

"Lies, you hardly have a bulge. You're a divine man. Eddy?"

"Yes?"

"Do you want to share the treasure with Charlie?"

She had her mouth pressed against his chest and he was brushing his teeth. "What was that?"

"If you want to share the treasure."

"Yes, with you."

"Not with Charlie?"

He took the toothbrush out of his mouth. "Shouldn't I? He's the only one who can take us to von Wittenberg."

155

She put her hands against his ribs and pushed. He didn't budge. "Eddy, I want to be rid of Charlie."

"A divorce you mean?"

"Yes, that too."

"Does he know?"

"He should by now, but we haven't really discussed it."

"And what do you intend to do afterward?"

She pursed her mouth. "Isn't that rather up to you?"

He wrapped a towel around his waist, padded after her into the kitchen, and watched her while she made breakfast. She leaned against him for a moment. "Eddy, I don't think that Charlie should have any part of that gold. He's a nasty little man."

"How would you cut him out?"

She smiled. "The secret is in the rivers, isn't it? The Vechta and the Hase?"

"The bacon is burning."

She took the pan off the stove. "Why don't you tell him that they are different rivers, then there's nothing he can do, even if he does manage to copy the map."

Eddy nodded. "If you like."

She poured coffee while he ate. "I'll bring you Charlie's atlas, there must be lots of rivers in Germany."

"No need, I'll call them the Ems and the Werse, near Münster."

She kissed his cheek. "You're so clever."

"I rode a bus up and down Germany for years. But don't you think Charlie'll go after us when he finds out?"

She struck a match and blew it out elegantly after he'd lit his cigarette, dropping it tenderly into the ashtray. "We'll be very rich by then, we can hire bodyguards. And if he gets too bothersome . . ."

Eddy finished his coffee. "Then what?"

"*Pow!*" Viola leaned across the table. "That's what."

*

Charlie leaned over the railing of the pavilion's balcony and stared into the water.

"Morning," Eddy said. "Viola asked me to bring you your breakfast. Here you are."

"Thank you. You can put it down over there."

"I would also like to talk to you."

Charlie stared dully at his visitor. "I wouldn't know what we could talk about. Or is this about Viola? You can take her with you, it doesn't seem like you need my permission."

"Eat your nice eggs," Eddy said. "The situation isn't as bad as you think. I want to talk to you about gold."

Charlie carried two chairs to the table. "You want to buy Viola?"

"Not today. Remember the Rembrandt I gave to you in Hamburg?"

Charlie chewed. "*Absalom?*"

"Is it in Paraguay now?"

"I don't see of what concern . . ."

Eddy raised his hand. "Easy, I helped you steal it."

"You didn't know," Charlie said, grinning, "you never suspected a thing."

"Is it in Paraguay or not?"

"It is, but that whole case is finished by statutes of limitation. Even the police don't care anymore."

"War crimes last forever."

Charlie wiped the last of his eggs with his toast. "Only in case of loss of life, and so far I have never had the pleasure of killing anyone." He looked up. "Say, do you know what struck me when we met that time? That you look like the joker in the painting. A remarkable likeness. Same facial characteristics and body posture. Same hair even, although yours isn't that long. Most remarkable." Charlie got up and went back to the railing. He looked over his shoulder when he heard Eddy's chair scrape on the floor. "Is that why you threw that bottle at the painting? Because I'm sure it was you, I never believed that story about the drunken French general."

"Maybe I did."

"Not that it matters now. What does matter?" Charlie observed

157

the quiet water of the pond. "Did Viola tell you I'm bankrupt?"

Eddy walked back to the table. "Yes. Come back and sit down. I can't talk to you when you turn your back to me."

Charlie pushed himself free of the balustrade. "All right, but I won't listen unless I can make a lot of money on the deal."

"Millions."

"If you're going to pull my leg . . ."

Eddy offered a cigarette. "I'm serious, millions."

"Lire?"

"Dollars, pounds, dinars, whatever currency you can name."

"Ha!"

"Listen."

Charlie listened. "I don't believe you. The tale is outrageous."

"Now why," Eddy asked, "should I invent such a story, and why would Kroll? Kroll was no fool."

Charlie cackled. "Foolish enough to let himself be killed by his old pal."

"I didn't intend to do away with him."

"He didn't intend to," Charlie said softly, "he just sort of shoved the fellow into a truck. Okay. So it's all true, a gold mine waits between the Ems and the Werse, even better, the gold is already packed. All you need is a spade and a truck. Now what do you want of me?"

"Take me to von Wittenberg."

Charlie peered into his cup. "I could use more coffee. Sure, I can take you to von Wittenberg, no problem at all." He poked his finger at Eddy. "Just come up with a little more encouragement. I would love to believe in the quest."

"You get half of the gold."

"That'll be later, what do I get now?"

"A trip to Paraguay."

Charlie groaned. "Just what I need. At your expense?"

Eddy patted his jacket. "I'm carrying my life's savings."

"How much?"

"About five thousand dollars."

Charlie shook his head. "Hardly enough. I like to travel first class and Viola will be going too."

"The car?" Eddy asked.

Charlie got up. "Let's go to the house. The car is in Kroll's name?"

"Yes."

"I saw the car," Charlie said, "luxury model, automatic, low mileage. Hmm."

"Worth twenty thousand."

Charlie sneered. "A stolen car? Maybe half. Will you let me sell it?"

"Sure."

They walked back to the house. Charlie touched Eddy's arm. "Okay, on two conditions."

Eddy waited.

Charlie put up a finger. "One, you pay for the trip and I handle the money."

"Yes."

"Two, until we dig up the gold and share it Viola is mine. She sleeps with me."

Eddy admired a rosebush. "Anything you say."

Charlie extended his right hand. Eddy shook it. Charlie jerked it back. "What are you doing now?"

Eddy looked surprised too. "Didn't you want to shake my hand?"

"Of course not, I wanted the car keys."

Eddy handed them over and Charlie slipped them into his pocket. "Shaking hands," he muttered, "really."

Charlie walked between two rows of cedar bushes cut into animal shapes. Two young men kept pace at his sides. They had popped up as he'd gotten out of the car, like robots, alerted by a silent warning system. Somewhere, Charlie thought, a shapeless Neapolitan mother-machine, energized on spaghetti and tomato sauce, poops them out. Once a year Filippo comes to reap the harvest. He takes them to an electronic greenhouse and they grow. Before he takes them out he has their heads opened to program them, so that they'll behave according to the code of the Mafia. It's not necessary for them to talk; maybe this lot is speechless too.

"What lovely bushes these are. Did you make the deer and foxes?"

"*Prego?*"

Charlie pointed at the small cedar trees.

"No, Capo Filippo likes to do it himself, but we are sometimes allowed to help."

Capo Filippo was waiting in his back garden, communing with azaleas that exploded in bright colors. The young men stayed back near the fence, each under his own pillar supporting a stone head of a warrior, overgrown with lichen and moss. Charlie walked on. Behind him the bodyguards dangled their hands, their fingers somewhat bent, ready to catch and to throttle. "Signore

Vrieslander," Capo Filippo said, "good afternoon to you. It is a good afternoon because the sun is out again."

Charlie knelt on the gravel.

Capo Filippo produced his right hand from behind his back, studied it for a moment, and then held it in front of Charlie's mouth. Monkey, Charlie thought. Filthy baboon. Infected asshole. He formulated his definitions solemnly, then kissed the hand that floated quietly in space.

He got up again.

"A favor?" asked Capo Filippo.

"A favor."

"Walk with me a little and enjoy the flowers. We aren't young anymore, Signore Vrieslander, and the pleasures of old men are simple. The work is done but we still live on for a while and enjoy ourselves in peace. Azaleas have expressive blooms, don't you agree?"

"Yes, Capo Filippo."

"You also have a beautiful garden, I believe, but you got rid of your house."

Charlie spread his hands. "I had bad luck, and heavy debts."

"Not anymore?"

"I'm no longer solvent."

Capo Filippo nodded. "A curse that struck me too once. I was a greengrocer then. But it was an illusion."

"Your store wasn't real?"

Capo Filippo shuffled on slowly. "No, that store did exist, and so did my vegetables." His hands formed a ball. "Cabbages with crisp curling leaves." His fingers approached each other and gestured away again, drawing different shapes in the air. "Carrots, leeks, artichokes. The bankruptcy was an illusion. Every ending is no more than a fresh beginning, Signore Vrieslander. After that I sold produce from a street stall, a little later I controlled the market." He smiled softly. "Others now do that for me, and I returned to where I started. I'm a gardener again."

"I made a fresh start too, Capo Filippo."

"And I can be of help in your activity?"

"Capo Filippo," Charlie said bravely, "I never disappointed you, my dealings with you were pure."

"You repaid my money," Capo Filippo said, "but I did not charge you interest for the time that you used my energy."

Charlie bowed his head.

"Had you forgotten?" the old man whispered.

"I had."

"Forget it again. Was that the favor?"

"I thank you," Charlie said.

Capo Filippo picked a flower and stuck it carefully into Charlie's buttonhole. "That was not the favor you came for. What is it that keeps you active now?"

"Some new business."

"That's good. Here in Italy?"

"In South America."

"That's better. If you make money in this country the bank will take it away from you."

"But I need a little capital for expenses," Charlie said.

"How much?"

"I brought you an almost new Mercedes. I need as much as you will give me for it."

"The car is on the other side of the house?"

"Yes, Capo Filippo."

Capo Filippo's fingers clicked. The bodyguards under the antique Roman heads straightened up. "Romero, fetch Signore Vrieslander's car."

Romero caught the keys, sprinted away, and returned within seconds behind the wheel of the large car. Capo Filippo turned to Charlie. "The car is yours?"

"No. It belonged to a German. The German died two days ago, run down by a truck in the red-light quarter of Frankfurt. The truck drove on."

"The German was drunk?"

"Yes, Capo Filippo."

"Any witnesses?"

"The accident happened at four in the morning, the only witness is the man who brought me the car, a good friend of my wife."

"Reliable?"

"Yes, Capo Filippo. He is my partner, we will go to South America together."

"Romero," Capo Filippo said, "fetch ten thousand dollars in small bills." He looked at his watch. "There is time for a glass of wine, Signore Vrieslander." His thin hand supported Charlie's elbow as he directed his guest.

They faced each other in a vast room. On a rosewood side table stood an antique set of scales. Charlie admired the instrument.

"You said you have a partner in your new venture?" Capo Filippo asked.

"Yes."

"You are in balance?"

"We are, it's a fifty-fifty deal."

The Capo picked up two equal weights and placed one on each balance. "Not always a wise choice." He flicked the scales, making them swing wildly. "It suspends you both." He poured the wine and gave Charlie a glass. "Red wine, Signore Vrieslander, the color of your blood."

They drank.

Capo Filippo's eyes twinkled. "And of his, your wife's friend's. Does death frighten you, Signore Vrieslander?"

"Yes," Charlie said.

"That's good. The fear of death makes us live on."

"**D**o you have everything?" Viola asked. "Whatever you don't take now is lost forever." She made a pretty picture — a slender, dark-haired elf perched on the windowsill, dressed in a Dior robe.

"Could you sound a little less cheerful?" Charlie asked.

"What am I doing wrong now?" she said, still in the same merry voice, blowing a kiss at Eddy over Charlie's shoulder.

Charlie knelt on the lid of his suitcase, intent on manipulating its locks. "You sound too damned happy. I gave you a marvelous time here, are you so glad it's all over?"

Viola gathered up her gown and slid down from the window. She sat on the suitcase. "*You* had a marvelous time here, all I had to do was fit in with your moods. Now try." The locks snapped shut.

"Shit." Charlie held up a pistol. "I forgot to put it in."

"Leave it here, you'll never get it through the airport's checkpoint."

"Leave my Walther here? Are you crazy? Over four hundred dollars, double that if I'd bought it in a store."

Eddy lifted his legs off the couch. "Put it in my case, I have plenty of room. They hardly ever look in carry-on luggage these days."

Viola jumped up. "You're not taking any firearms. If we are stopped, we can forget about the whole thing."

Charlie looked at Eddy. "Do you have a weapon?"

"Yes," Viola said, "in his fly."

Charlie's fingers tapped jerkily on the pistol's holster. "I do wish you weren't so foul-mouthed."

Viola smiled sweetly. "Prick prick prick," she sang, "that's all you ever think of. Eddy does have a gun in his fly, I was merely stating a fact. He's showed it to me often enough."

Charlie's face worked. "She's right," Eddy said soothingly, "but it's only a little gun."

"Big enough." Viola studied her nails.

Charlie straightened out slowly. "I've had enough of this."

Eddy turned around and pulled the revolver out of his trousers. He zipped his fly again and showed Charlie the gun.

"Give," Viola said, "you too, Charlie. I'll throw them into the pond."

"No," Eddy said.

"Why not?"

"It's been with me for a long time," Eddy said, "I don't want it to rot away here."

"A fetish, is it?" Viola sat primly on the couch, resting her firm little chin daintily on a slender bent hand. "You feel that way about the Walther too, Charlie?"

"Of course. A man needs his gun."

"Nonsense, men carry little pocketknives nowadays."

"Not real men."

She bent down, displaying her cleavage. "You claim to be a real man?"

Charlie glared. "It could be she's right," Eddy said. "Maybe we should leave our guns. Can we wrap them up and bury them anywhere?"

Viola dropped her sexy act and walked to the window. "A pity the moon isn't full." She turned round. "But it's waxing again so it'll be of some help. My herbs are in bloom now so the spell should be potent. Some objects are strong in their spirit. I can stage a proper ceremony and you can use the box I have buried under my moon stone. The guns will rest there but their strength will follow us."

Charlie picked up his pistol and struggled to his feet. "Bah."

"A hole is a hole," Eddy said. "Viola's garden would be a good place, at least we'll remember the spot."

Charlie and Eddy had pulled the large center stone away and were digging while Viola tripped from one cedar stump to the next, her sleeves fluttering as she sang in a shrill voice. Charlie rested on his spade. "Stop making a spectacle of yourself."

She clawed at the air and bared her perfect teeth. "Shshsh, you're interrupting my secret chant."

Eddy bent down and picked up a metal box. A crude picture of a naked girl riding a broom had been painted on its lid. He shook the dirt off and showed it to Charlie. Viola pushed in between the two men. She opened the box and picked up a small bundle that she stuck in the sash of her robe.

"What's that?" Charlie asked.

"It's mine. Wait here, I'll bring your guns."

She came back. "I thought of everything. I wrapped them in plastic so they won't rust, I even rubbed them with oil. Here you are, now say good-bye to them." She turned her back. "They can rest in each other's arms."

Charlie held his pistol. The plastic film protecting the gun was thin, his finger was close to the trigger. His thumb pressed the safety latch. His hand moved a little, the pistol pointed at Eddy.

Eddy's revolver moved too.

"Are you aiming at me?" Charlie asked. "This thing fires quickly."

Eddy pushed the open box with his foot. His voice was gentle. "Please drop it, Charlie."

The pistol fell. Eddy bent down and placed his revolver next to it. He closed the lid.

"All done?" Viola asked.

Eddy shoveled the dirt back into the hole.

"Replace the stone carefully." She had brought her spade and dug out some little plants, pushing them around the glistening rock. "Creeping thyme, it grows quickly, no one'll suspect that the stone was moved."

Charlie walked away. Viola linked her arm into Eddy's. "Fool."

"Perhaps," Eddy said. "Your showdown isn't mine."

"I love you, you should have trusted me."

"Wasn't the Walther loaded?"

"Of course not. I emptied out the clip."

Eddy shook his head.

She tore her arm free and held up the little bundle, whispering at it fiercely. "You failed me. Why?"

"Where's Viola?" Charlie asked when Eddy came into the room. "Did you bury her too?" He opened the window and looked out. Viola's lament drifted into the room. "Crazy bitch, leaping about and wailing. Just look at her."

Eddy held up a bottle. "A last drink before you call the cab?"

The strain of the last few days had been too much for Charlie. He didn't see the glass Eddy tried to give him. His teeth chattered.

"Charlie?"

Charlie's small fists rattled on Eddy's chest. "They set me up, the bastards!"

Eddy stepped back. The glass broke on the floor. "Easy now."

"The hell with them," Charlie shouted. "But the gold will set me free."

Viola came in, looking quite calm. "Stop shouting, Charlie. Shouldn't we go? There isn't all that much time."

Bogotá, Colombia

"Eldorado, land of gold," the stewardess intoned solemnly through the jet's loudspeakers. The plane circled above Colombia's sprawling capital. "We'll be landing within a few minutes."

Eddy looked down at the plateau, extending to faraway clouds stuck on mountain peaks marking its boundaries. A dirty fog dimmed the contours of Bogotá's creeping traffic that filled every street. When the plane banked he saw suburbs dotted with the hard chlorinated blue of private swimming pools set in gardens of spacious homes, surrounded by lush trees. The jet crossed the center again; the city's other side consisted of countless shacks forming a spreading sore of soggy cartons and dented tinplate, reaching out to contaminate farmland and fields of pale green shrubs.

"Like it?" Charlie asked.

"No."

"Paraguay is worse, but this is where we will find von Wittenberg, safely tucked away in the care of his medical priest."

Viola smiled at customs officers, small men with liquid eyes and trim mustaches. They waved her through, staring at her legs. The immigration officer perused the gentle uplift of her breasts before he stamped her passport with a flourish.

The road leading from the airport cut cleanly through mud-

168

flats built up in parts with sagging structures of unfinished and abandoned skyscrapers — dead and transparent hulks only partly screened by lurid billboards. A limousine honked its two-toned horn at an Indian woman trailing a donkey heavily loaded with rotten boards. She wore a man's hat and a formless black dress; dried-up clay flaked off her bare shins. Ahead the clouds slowly picked up color, becoming burning garlands hung about a dark shrine, until their flames licked down and set the hilltops on fire.

More donkeys blocked the road and plodded in the dust, too lethargic to respond to their masters' whips. The cab driver edged through the dark mass, banging the outside of his door with his flat hand.

Night fell as the cab entered Bogotá, in the wake of two buses driving abreast. A third overtook them, careening onto the sidewalk, and the cab followed its example. A policeman blew his whistle. The cab driver lifted two fingers. *"Hijo de puta."* He spat out of the window.

Little boys riding the bus's rear bumper were thrown off by a jolt and scampered about. The cab missed them, but metal screeched as its fender scraped a lamp post. Charlie cursed; the driver shrugged and referred to the mother of God.

"If we ever make it to the hotel," Eddy said, "I could do with some sleep."

Their rooms were connected and Viola wandered in while Eddy unpacked his bag. She inspected the bed. Charlie came in too. "We're just in time. The Freiherr isn't doing well but the doctor says I can see him, I should phone again tomorrow."

Voices of street vendors interrupted Eddy's sleep. A nearby churchtower dominated the clamor of jukeboxes in the cafés crowding its base by playing a carillon amplified from well-worn tapes.

Eddy drifted off again into dreams of small gnarled faces, the masks of gnomes that whispered murderous advice. He tried to kick the annoying apparitions aside, but their spindly hands gripped his ankles. He found himself in a forest glade tinged with morose, off-white colors where, not surprisingly, Charlie was tied

169

to a stump. The gnomes pushed on, explaining Charlie's weaknesses which, if properly played on, would make it more fun to torture him. "Afterward we'll help you slit his throat," a female form screeched, offering a dagger. Eddy seized her arm and bent it back but it was made of wood that, though appearing quite brittle, wouldn't snap. Her mate was still clutching his leg.

Eddy half woke as he fought the demons; the hellish scene faded and almost became a hotel room again, but the creaking and rattling of heating tubes buried in the walls snaked around him, dragging him back down. Eddy struggled but the dream only shattered when cars collided just under his window.

Eddy stumbled through the room, looking for a light switch. He dropped his cigarette on the bed and felt around for it. His fingers touched a bulge and located its origin under the mattress. The bundle stuck between the metal coils of the bed's frame seemed familiar. It came undone in his hand, and two misshapen roots fell out of their cotton wrap on which a naked girl aloft on a broomstick was crudely drawn in ink. The roots' semihuman shapes were intertwined but popped free as he pulled. He grunted admiringly as he felt their tiny arms and legs, and the male's minute penis, complete with hairs sprouting from its end, that had been stuck in the female's crotch. How intimate had been their embrace, how deftly created these totems were, how perfectly their contorted torsos had grown cruelly slanted eyes and puckered mouths, invoked by Viola's chants in the Empoli garden.

The room had grown cold and his body was so shaken that he had to rub his legs before he could stand on them. It was an effort to fetch a metal wastebasket from the bathroom and tear off toilet paper that kept on slipping from his grip. There wasn't much of it; he hunted about for more but there was only the Bible on his night table. The roots, wrapped in holy words ignited by his lighter, smouldered slowly in the tin trash can. Acrid smoke swirling up made him cough. He opened a window and wafted the stench away with a towel.

When the figures were reduced to ash he flushed them away and flopped back on the bed, planning to use his will to keep future disturbances out, but images formed again. The hidden cache of Nazi gold soothed his fears. In timeless flashes he possessed the treasure and luxuriated in a palm-shaded mansion, until the villa's driveway became a maze attempting to trap him, and a sports car he had just bought sank out of sight, leaving a bubble that stank when it burst.

Viola entered the dream, radiating beauty, as lovely and unspoiled by associations as when he first met her in Florence. Eddy ran up to her, babbling about secrets they were to share, the glorious feats they would achieve together. She walked by him, staring straight ahead. He wanted to leap after her but his hair was caught in a tree.

When Viola came into the room she found him twisted in his sheets, snoring stupidly. She slipped her hand under the mattress. "Eddy?"

He didn't see her clearly at first and groped for his reading glasses.

"What did you do with them, they aren't here." She held up the empty wrap.

"The gnomes?"

"My henbane roots."

He sat up. "You should keep your shit to yourself. I burned them."

"*No*. They were to work for both of us."

"I think," Eddy said, "that I'm sick. Why don't you go away, I'll come down later."

He vomited in the bathroom after she left and went back to bed. The Bible's remains stuck out of the half-open drawer and he pulled them out. Part of the Old Testament was still intact. He found Absalom in the index, Samuel, chapters 13 to 19, and glanced through the closely printed pages. A few lines stained by the imprint of a coffee cup caught his attention ... *from the soles of his feet even to the crown of his head there was no blemish in him. And when he cut his hair he weighed it and it weighed two hundred shekels.*

He dropped the book back and slammed the drawer.

Charlie waved at him in the hotel's lobby. "Good news, the Freiherr will see me tomorrow morning. Care to join me for lunch?"

Eddy rubbed his stomach. "I had a little trouble last night, maybe the oysters they served on the plane. Were you all right?"

Charlie beamed. "Fit as a fiddle."

Eddy walked down a busy avenue, looking for a barbershop.

"A little off the top, sir?"

"No, short please."

"How short?"

Eddy looked out of the window. A soldier waiting at a bus stop took off his cap and scratched his skull. "As short as that man over there."

The barber made his scissors bite the air. "As you wish, señor, the customer is king."

"Maybe I picked the wrong hotel," Charlie said. "Were you afflicted with lice, Eddy?"

Viola turned away and covered her eyes. "Oh *no*."

Eddy sat down. "It'll grow again. Been here long?"

"Too long, and Charlie got himself drunk." Her hand caressed Eddy's. "Now what did you do that for?"

The bar's peculiar lighting transformed Charlie's mouth into a toothless cavity, his red nose poked aggressively from sunken cheeks. "She doesn't go for shiny skulls, it's all up with you, lover boy."

Viola patted her husband's head. "Contain your jealousy, my bald little dwarf." Her nails pressed down, he pushed her hand away. "Ouch."

"A drink," Eddy said. "Can I get you one too?"

Charlie was still rubbing his head. "Rum for me, and as I'm paying I'll order."

Viola poked at Charlie's stomach. "My bald little dwarf with his big round tum. And whose money is he spending?"

"Double rum," Charlie told the bartender, "same for her."

"Soda water," Eddy said.

"Still not feeling well?" Viola asked.

"Much better, it probably was the altitude, we're nine thousand feet up here."

Viola held up her glass. "To my protector's health."

Charlie replaced his drink. "No."

Viola insisted. "To my lover who is financing this expedition and who will release us all from suffering."

"Never." Charlie raised his voice. "To von Wittenberg."

"I don't care for German generals," Eddy said.

Charlie leaned around Viola. "No-good Nazis?"

"That's right."

Charlie leered. "You're no-good either. I knew that when I saw you thirty years ago, prancing about in your tailor-made uniform in that whorehouse at the Kleine Alster, and I'm sure you weren't any good before that." He took a sip. "Or after."

Viola sighed. "A tailor-made uniform. My saint in armor."

"Saint, ha, he conjures up demons. What about the Obersturmbahnführer, lover boy? You told me that tale yourself. What did you extort from Kroll in return for his freedom?"

Eddy drank his soda water.

"Well?"

"A promise."

"Did he keep it?"

"Yes."

"So the no-good Nazi was reliable?"

"Yes."

"But you pushed him under a truck." Charlie's finger jabbed accusingly. "Maybe he shouldn't have trusted *you*. So why should I? Who says you won't kill me too when the time comes. When we dig for gold between your famous rivers?"

Eddy drank more soda water.

"What do you say to that, lover boy?"

"I have something to say," Eddy said.

Charlie put up his fists. "Let's have it."

"I've cheated you both."

"Both?" Viola whispered.

The bartender came by. Eddy asked for whiskey. "I thought I was being clever but now it all seems different . . . and useless."

Charlie thumped the counter. "You're not going to convince

174

me that the treasure isn't there. It *has* to be. Why would you have brought us all the way out here if there's nothing to it?"

"I believe that the treasure is there."

"If you're trying to be funny," Viola said, "you're not doing too well."

Eddy smiled. "Don't get upset. I didn't have much confidence in either of you. I misnamed the rivers."

"The Vechta and the Hase?" Viola asked.

"The Ems and the Werse?" Charlie asked.

"The Aue and the Leda."

Charlie sat back on his stool. "Or the Meuse and the Rhine. You can play that game forever."

Eddy pushed his glass across the bar. "Same again please. No, the Aue and the Leda. I may as well tell you, now that we've gone some of the way together."

"Why lie to me?" Viola asked. "I'm *with* you."

"So you say."

"You trust me now?"

"No."

He caught her wrist easily as she tried to slap his face. "Let go, you're hurting me."

"Sure."

Her hand came up again. Eddy shook his head. "Don't. I don't trust myself either, but I know now that I don't really want all that loot for myself." He looked at Charlie. "It's better to share. The worst part of the trip is still to come, maybe it'll be easier if we can be open with each other."

Viola hissed with rage. "Idiot. Don't you *care* anymore?"

Eddy pushed her hand down gently. "Sure I care, the gold will recharge me again."

"More rum," Charlie said.

"To the three of us, whether we fail or win."

Charlie drank. "Yes, but why you suddenly have to be all honesty is beyond me. All games are crooked."

"There we go again," Viola said. "Straight lines don't exist, why try to improve on nature?" She swept her arm, knocking her drink off the table. "The great Vrieslander dogma."

Eddy was on his third glass. The whirling of approaching drunkenness was clearly noticeable already, his thoughts flashed at increased speed and became impulses that were hard to hold back. He wanted to sit between Viola and Charlie, embrace them both, and warn them against their own foolish greed. For a moment he thought about love, and what the term might imply.

Charlie left the bar and stood near an electric piano that had been providing background music. He beat time with his glass and some of his drink spilled and leaked along the instrument's open lid. The pianist, a white-haired man, lifted his hands from the keyboard and berated Charlie in guttural German. Viola's breast rubbed against Eddy's arm. "I want to go to bed. Are you taking me upstairs?"

Eddy thoughtfully stirred his drink.

"Darling?"

"No, I think I'll go for a walk."

She got up shakily. "Men. They're never there when you need them. Doesn't matter how many you collect."

Charlie came back. "The old fool wanted money to have his rotten piano repaired."

"Did you give it to him?"

"Me?"

"Eddy wants to go out." Viola smiled disdainfully. "And I'm tired. You better come with me if you want to stay out of trouble."

Charlie talked to the mirror behind the bar. "Lover boy, better be careful, Bogotá women have a bad reputation, you might get sick."

Viola kissed Charlie's cheek. "You aren't worried I might pass it to you, are you?"

"Sleep well," Eddy said, "see you at breakfast."

Eddy had been walking about for nearly an hour when a sad-eyed elderly man in a well-worn dark suit put himself in his way. "A lovely evening, señor."

"So it is."

The man carried a silver-knobbed cane and used it to point at a church. "The cathedral, and this is the famous Plaza Bolívar. A historical site, señor, a holy place, even the Chibchas thought it so."

"The Indians?"

"They had their pueblo here, around the temple that de Quesada burned and looted, for he had no use for beauty. He only came for gold, at the head of just two hundred men who staggered in their armor through jungle and mountain passes for several years. The sixteenth century, señor."

Eddy listened to the kindly voice, but a glint in the man's eyes made him aware of a shadow slinking behind. He whirled around and saw a young man run away. Eddy caught him easily. The young man dropped money; Eddy touched it with his foot. "Did you take that from me?"

"No, señor, it is mine."

Eddy twisted his prisoner's arm so that he had to bend down. "Pick it up and show it to me."

"You're causing me pain."

Eddy looked at the small wad the man held up. "Take off the rubber band." A single peso note neatly covered cut newsprint. "Old trick, eh? You were going to pickpocket me and exchange that for my cash."

"Let me go."

The other man approached. "Let go of my son or I'll call the police."

Two policemen approached from the far side of the square, trailing prostitutes and pointing out their attractions with their nightsticks.

"Go right ahead."

The old man balanced his stick in two hands. His chin came up. "I will defend my son, señor."

"No need." Eddy pushed his quarry to a stone bench. "Sit down and tell me what you had in mind. I won't tell the police."

The father sat on Eddy's other side. "You were right, señor, we are indeed thieves." His bloodshot eyes peered over his half-glasses. "My son and I work together. I will engage the foreign tourist of my choice or even bump him if he doesn't care for conversation. Once his attention is distracted my son goes through his pockets."

The son rubbed his arm. "*El cliente* will not notice that anything is amiss until it is too late."

Eddy offered cigarettes. "Your act did not work out tonight."

The father lit a match and cupped its flame solicitously while Eddy bent toward it. "We are usually quite successful. You were too observant. Have you been robbed before perhaps?"

"Not in this way."

The young man bowed shyly. "*Mis felicitaciones,* señor, perhaps you will join us for a drink?"

Eddy sipped his *aguardiente* under the torn awning of a street café.

"That one," the son said, "Papa?"

The father got up hurriedly. "Would you excuse us for a moment?"

The sidewalk was crowded and Eddy had trouble following the

performance. *El cliente* seemed to be a German, a substantial-looking man, crossbanded with camera and light meter and wearing an old-fashioned felt hat. The father zigzagged through the crowd and pulled up in front so suddenly that the tourist walked into him. The old man staggered and nearly fell. The German apologized while the son's hand crept under his jacket.

"Well done," Eddy said when the son joined him again. "Very deft."

"*Gracias,* señor, my father will be back in a minute. He will accompany our benefactor to the end of the block, pointing out sights."

"You both seem educated men."

"Father is a retired schoolteacher, but his pension is a pittance and I can't find work although I studied well."

"You speak good English."

The father sat down. "Knowledge is part of our trade. I also speak some German, are you from there?"

"No."

The old man looked at Eddy closely. "You remind me of someone I saw in an illustration; Siegfried, a shining god riding a carriage made of human bones. I was mistaken in thinking that I could deal with you."

"You have read widely."

"Bogotá, señor, is the Athens of South America."

The German's wallet was well filled, and Eddy's new-found friends invited him to dinner and led Eddy through alleys so steep that the absence of traffic allowed flowering weeds to grow between the cobblestones. In a restaurant hidden behind crumbling walls the Colombians got drunk. The son sang and the father recited poetry while the waitresses played guitars and danced. Eddy's nausea returned, so he thanked his happy hosts and took his leave.

He hesitated in the passage outside where, above the dark roofs, sharply silhouetted mountain peaks made their presence felt. To go back to the city's foul smell below was not a tempting choice.

The stars pulsated in thin clear air that smoothed the waves in his stomach. Eddy climbed on until he reached fields rising to the foothills. He sat on a rock, close to a shack. Its door was open and a fire burned inside; he thought he could smell incense. A young woman came out. Her dress was thin and her body clearly visible against the flickering light of flaming wood scraps. She had Viola's short black hair.

Eddy smiled. She raised her arms and pirouetted slowly. He raised his arm to greet her and got up to walk away.

"Señor?" the woman shrieked. "Fucky fucky?"

"No thanks." He walked further into the field, resisting the urge to run as her shrill voice cursed him.

Close to the hills silent black shapes suddenly rose into the air before him. The furious birds, larger than crows but shaped more deadly, had naked heads and curved beaks, as yellow as their legs tucked stiffly under black wings. Ahead an animal's carcass was a pale blotch against the dark earth. Eddy watched as its side bulged and heaved. A last bird hopped away from a gaping hole beneath the corpse's tail and flapped silently away, merging with the darkness of the mountains and the moonless night.

Eddy walked back a little and waited patiently under a tree. Soon the birds were back, feeding ravenously. He listened as their beaks tore at the carrion, snapping against bone. The pale shape trembled under the onslaught of the many scavengers working quickly and easily.

The power of a plodding beast now makes birds soar, Eddy thought. Who is the donkey? Am I the bird?

The night seemed darker now. He turned slowly and looked at the lights of the city far below. Then he began to walk away, moving faster and faster, running in fear. Was he now using the strength of the men he had killed?

The faces of the dead leered at him out of the darkness until he reached Bogotá's winding lanes. There he slowed, but the fear refused to evaporate, even when he reached his hotel.

A whiff of gin, the fragrance of good cigars — Charlie approved immediately. He despised the sickly smell of steamed food that hung in the clinic's corridor and cared little for the male nurse who ushered him into von Wittenberg's room.

"*Que entre,* señor," the Indian said. The small neat man was too unapproachable within his defense of tight brown skin and sleek black hair.

He left, but a second guard was stationed on a low chair just inside the door, hidden by a newspaper.

"Morning."

The paper creaked in response, then hinged forward. A well-dressed man jumped to his feet and clicked his heels. "Fauster."

"Vrieslander. I was told the Freiherr would receive me."

Fauster indicated white curtains in the room's rear. "The doctor is due any minute, perhaps we should wait. A drink?"

"A little early but I'll have one all the same." Charlie admired Fauster's brocade waistcoat and immaculate cuffs. Once a Prussian officer, now a caballero. They say, Charlie thought, that German shepherds turned loose in tropical jungle change into splendid wolves. It is indeed marvelous what a change of climate can do for looks.

"How is the general doing?"

Fauster blew a kiss to the forbidding curtains. "Badly. Gin?"

"Rum if I may."

"You're not from here I see." Fauster's eyes wandered over an array of bottles displayed on a side table. "I don't have it. Sorry."

"Gin, please. What's wrong with rum?"

Fauster pulled a tray of ice cubes from a small refrigerator stuck between the table's legs. "A drink for swine."

"I beg your pardon?" Charlie asked.

"Locals." Fauster twiddled his fingers disdainfully. "Cheap stuff, for Colombian street bums and democratic duds. Tonic with it?"

"Yes, please."

Fauster read the label on the small tonic bottle. "Aha, see? I was right again. Imported, proves how *dumm* the *Dummkopfen* are. Made in Venezuela with locally grown quinine. Your health."

"Are you a friend of the Freiherr?"

Fauster grunted in his glass. "No. His subordinate. I'm here in my official capacity, under Herr President's orders."

"The president of Colombia?"

The question amused Fauster. "I don't even know that fellow's name. No no, the president of Paraguay."

Charlie remembered the patient's presence and dropped his voice. "I'm so glad I came in time."

"You came to say good-bye?"

"And to make a request."

"The request may come too late," Fauster said, "the general will not speak again. It's amazing what hypnosis coupled to some understanding of modern medicine can do, but there are certain limits it seems."

"He is that ill?"

"The general has been in a coma for the last few days." Fauster got up. "The doctors are late, you may as well take a look."

Charlie peeked through the curtains and saw a snoring skull covered by dry skin. The nozzle from an oxygen tube penetrated into one nostril, held in place by a swatch of white adhesive.

"Here we are," Fauster said briskly.

An imposing figure with a walnut-colored, hook-nosed face came in, leading a small procession of white-coated men. His sharp eyes rested on Charlie.

Fauster stepped forward. "Allow me to introduce a foreign visitor, Padre Gomez."

Gomez's chin cut into his priestly collar. *"Buenos días."*

Charlie nodded. The padre paused, waiting for his assistants to line up behind him. The cortege proceeded rhythmically and began a vocal whine.

"Clowns," Fauster whispered to Charlie. "But effective, and holy of course. Listen."

The doctors' chant filled the room. "Mmmm, *Dios,* mmmm, *Madre Santa."*

"Gomez is a shaman," Fauster explained, "with a minor M.D. A little local sorcery blessed by Rome and mixed with empiricism goes a long way in this country."

"They just sing and dance around?"

"There's more to it."

Fauster marched back to the bed, doing his best not to be caught up in the synchronized line dance slowly approaching the patient. The screens slid away and revealed von Wittenberg's emaciated body, dressed in a loincloth and surrounded by a complicated system of transparent tubes terminating in various veins and orifices. A small electric pump hummed and sputtered; air globules bubbled in the pipes. The doctors formed a semicircle. The chant slowed down and became a litany; "Tem-tay tem-tay tem-tay TEM-tay." Fauster winked at Charlie and bent over to whisper into his ear. "A musical mantra with medicinal overtones, losing its strength unfortunately."

The doctors set to work; they seemed to be probing the general's body openings using a variety of plastic and stainless steel instruments. Vomit flushed Charlie's tongue; he burped painfully.

"Vayase, señor."

"What's that?"

"The padre wants you to leave. Let's finish our drinks."

"Yes." Charlie sat down and breathed deeply. "Listen, Herr Fauster. The Dutch government sent me on a special mission."

"To do with art?" Fauster asked. "I remember your name now, the Freiherr mentioned you once or twice. Are you buying or selling?"

"Neither. There will be a Rembrandt festival in Amsterdam and a book showing his collected works is being sponsored by our queen. The Freiherr owns Rembrandt's portrait of Absalom of which no reproductions are available."

"The Freiherr cannot help you anymore."

"Perhaps your good self . . ."

"Perhaps my good self," Fauster agreed. "The very person you should be looking for. I helped to dispose of the Freiherr's possessions. The general no longer owns anything, you see."

"You're joking," Charlie said sharply. "The hacienda? His extensive collections?"

"All gone. Spent, or if you prefer a more truthful word, wasted."

"Impossible."

Fauster smiled. "Very possible, not every one of us knows how to relate income to expenditure. The general indulged in expensive hobbies. Flown-in female company doesn't come cheap these days, Herr Vrieslander, especially if one is foolish enough to marry the ladies and then to dispose of them again."

"So how come he's here? This treatment isn't free, is it?"

"Herr President is a magnanimous man who does not forget old friends." Fauster frowned while the doctors filed past, their coats flapping in unison. "Even so, this has been going on long enough. I don't believe in throwing our resources away. We aren't" — he coughed behind his hand "socialists."

"The Rembrandt is still in Asunción?"

Fauster shook his head.

"So where is it?"

"Your mission is government funded?"

Charlie smiled. "Certainly, if you would like to assist I'll be happy to discuss a way of reimbursing you."

The light glinted on Fauster's manicured nails. "I will not charge a fee for the honor of serving a queen, but it so happens that I may be in need of your services."

Charlie settled in his chair. "I'm yours."

"A small but valuable painting I'm getting rid of," Fauster said. "You see, the president doesn't care for it when he comes to visit and my lady friend claims the design reminds her of the kitchen tablecloth. A composition of lines, done by a countryman of yours."

"Mondrian," Charlie said. "What colors?"

"You are indeed an expert. Red, yellow, and blue."

"His later period. You have determined a price?"

"No, I think it should be auctioned privately."

"I will take care of the transaction," Charlie said brightly.

"At ten percent?"

"Twenty." Charlie gestured lightly. "Arrangements between auctioneers and their friends do not always benefit the seller, you need a trustworthy observer. Did you obtain the Mondrian during the war?"

"In 1943."

Charlie wrinkled his nose. "The wrong year, there may still be a search out for it, art collectors have long memories."

"The previous owner is dead."

"Records live on. Better leave the matter to me, Herr Fauster, I specialize in this field, as the Freiherr knows, I served him well."

Fauster's fingertips touched his chin.

"I usually charge more," Charlie said softly, "and eighty percent of an appreciable sum is more than a hundred percent of nothing."

"Leave me an address in Europe, I may have the painting delivered to you."

"Good, and the Rembrandt's whereabouts?"

"Nicaragua."

"The present owner?"

"The president of Nicaragua."

"Doesn't that country have a problem at the moment?"

Fauster nodded. "It does indeed, the country is a fortress right now and does not welcome strangers while it deals with the guerrillas. But I can get you there, Herr Vrieslander. Shall we say ten percent after all?"

The doctors had left. A painful gurgle behind the curtains made Fauster look up. When it changed into a dry rattle he pushed himself reluctantly out of his chair.

"Oh dear," Fauster said when he came back from the bed. He picked up a telephone. "Hello? *Urgencia.*" He replaced the receiver. "Well, Herr Vrieslander?"

"Ten percent," Charlie said. "The queen cannot be disappointed. I have to go at once."

"Come in," Fauster called and turned back to Charlie. "This is South America, everything can be arranged, and don't worry about your safety once you're there. Somoza is still in charge and he has powerful friends; we are concerned and so is the United States."

He frowned at the commotion around the bed. Padre Gomez raised a copper cross with both hands, murmuring musical Latin. The Indian nurse waved a censer with an ecstatic smile. Perfumed smoke drifted close; Fauster waved it away irritably.

*

"And?" Eddy asked.

Charlie rubbed his hands. "We're as good as there. The president of Nicaragua has the Rembrandt. A Paraguayan airplane carrying military supplies for Managua is due here later today to refuel. We'll be allowed on board. A certain Major Koboldski will meet us at Las Mercedes airport and arrange an introduction to Somoza.

"A Pole?" Eddy asked.

Charlie snarled at him. "I would say not." He brightened up again. "Many Germans have Polish names."

"How was the Freiherr?"

"What the hell do you care?"

186

Eddy smiled apologetically. "Didn't you say that he was rather ill?"

"He's now rather dead. Where's Viola?"

"I believe she has gone out for a walk."

"He believes," wailed Charlie. "And *she* is farting about. Do I have to take care of everything? The plane is due in a few hours."

Eddy turned away. "I'll find her, you go ahead and pack."

On his way to the elevator Charlie found himself surrounded by a crowd of Japanese. He struggled through it but made little headway and nearly fell over two identically dressed children. They smiled up at him.

"Cloned Chinks," Charlie shouted. The twins slid through the elevator door which closed after them in Charlie's face.

He was kicking the door when Viola and Eddy, arm in arm, joined him.

Nicaragua, 1980

Viola, tucked up in the large passenger's seat of the rented car, purred happily. Eddy ignored her, preferring to concentrate on the soft hiss of the Chrysler's tires. The limousine sped along the curving road. He held its wheel with two fingers and glanced at the luminescent dashboard. The needles trembling in the middle of their respective dials supported his sense of total control, not only of the car but also of the view — an expanse of metallic blue, bordered by sun-lined clouds and, lower down, swaying tropical foliage. Steady as she goes, he thought happily and moved his head slightly so that he could see his eyes in the rearview mirror. Clear blue steely eyes, keen, serious. He leaned back and smiled. For a moment he had identified with Captain Cook on the bridge of his valiant vessel, discovering Alaska. Eddy Sachs, at the wheel of a Chrysler convertible, discovering Nicaragua.

Viola's fingertips touched his wrist. "Where are we going?"

"To Las Mercedes. I was told they have a good bar at the airport, I thought we could have a drink there and then return to Managua." He could feel her nails and pulled his hand back; she reached out again.

"I want you to cuddle me."

He frowned, trying to recapture the sensation of courageous security that had been so intense just now. She lifted his arm and

188

nestled against him. "Isn't there a side road? With a little lake at the end? We could go for a swim."

"Sharks."

"What?"

"There are sharks here," he explained patiently, "freshwater sharks, most unusual, but all over the place in Nicaragua. Dangerous country, you know."

She giggled. "Oh, nonsense. We'll play Tarzan, you can swing through the mangrove trees and I'll watch you from the water. Me Jane."

"And guerrillas. The hotel manager said that they control most of the rural areas, wherever the National Guard can't easily follow them, but the roads are still okay. Didn't you see that armored car we just passed?"

"We're tourists, they need us for the money."

"The Russians give them money."

"Oh, never mind the silly Russians."

I'm Captain Cook, Eddy thought, and the passenger is irritating me, she'll have to walk the plank. He braked. The Chrysler had come up behind a jeep filled with soldiers trying to see in all directions at once, holding automatic rifles on which bayonets gleamed malevolently; the slow-moving vehicle looked like a moody porcupine with all its quills up.

Suddenly aware of the evil atmosphere surrounding the growling jeep, Viola pulled up her legs and embraced her knees. "Everybody is frightened here. I never want to know fear again. Safety can be bought." She uncurled again and stretched lazily. "We'll be incredibly wealthy soon, won't we, Eddy?"

"Yes." The jeep straddled the yellow line painted in the middle of the road. Eddy took his foot off the gas and listened to the automatic gears clicking down and the stronger hum of the engine.

Viola nodded. "I think we should live in the United States, on the California coast, and if we want to go anywhere we can fly from there and back again as soon as we're bored. They say you can get Mexican servants out there, lovely people who do as they're told. We'll have a swimming pool dug behind the house, with a high wall around it. I'll plant vines and creepers and won't wear any clothes during the day. At night I'll dress up in Parisian gowns, we'll rent good movies that we can show ourselves and we'll cut the bad parts and play the good parts again. Yes?"

"Good idea." Eddy passed the jeep. The driver, his face invisible under a heavy helmet, saluted by lifting his hand off the wheel. Eddy grinned and waved back. The Guardia is paid by Washington, Eddy thought, and we're in an American car. How nice to be with friends.

Viola misinterpreted his expression. "You fantasize too, don't you? Will you tell me?"

"Not now, I've got to watch the road, too many curves."

"Shall I tell you what Charlie is imagining?"

"Sure."

She sat back, puffing on her cigarette. "He plans to buy a Rolls-Royce, some old square convertible model. He'll be living on the Riviera, the French part because he never wants to see Italy again. And he'll have one of those large white plastic villas sitting on a hill, he likes his hills furry." She giggled.

Eddy glanced at her. "You like him again, do you?"

"I hate him, nasty little bastard. Furry hills, he has those weird expressions. He'll probably plant shrubs, but that's his other hobby. Every morning the Rolls is driven to his front door by a tall stately woman from the Congo, with upstanding breasts and black-blue skin, she's dressed in a white leather jumpsuit."

"Are you making that up?"

"No." Her mouth tightened. "He always talks about other women and about what he does to them or likes to do to them. Want to hear the rest of it?"

"Sure," he said again, wishing she wouldn't talk. The road was clear and cut through dense jungle, a hilltop ahead glistened in the fierce sunlight. The enormous leaves of parasitic plants climbing up the trunk of a palm moved as the car slid by; Eddy thought he saw brown hands and perhaps a head showing up against the trunk's light bark. A large monkey? Or a small sniper? He whistled out of tune and made up a song. "Man with a gun,

gun is fun." He wished he had his own and promised himself to make a special trip and dig it up someday.

"Are you listening?"

"Yes, I saw a monkey in a tree, I'm sorry, what happened to the Rolls?"

"That woman gets out of the car and stands at attention and then there is this sudden thunder of four large motorcycles roaring out of the garage, they park neatly around the Rolls, each one beside a fender. The bikes are also ridden by black women, same model as the driver, they're at least six feet tall and very supple and well formed; they line up to be inspected."

"By charming Charlie?"

"Yes. He struts up and examines them one by one, that part must come from the time when he was an officer serving with the British. He checks that the women are all in order, but they're not of course."

"They're disrespectful?"

"They wouldn't dare, but their breasts aren't sufficiently visible so he has to fiddle about with their zippers. A little up, a little down. That's a precision job and he has to take his time. Can you imagine Charlie standing on his toes? Little eager beaver? He's about to choke with excitement and eventually, after much touching and feeling, he approves and the female driver opens the door for him and lights his cigar. He waves it and the whole caboodle thunders down the driveway, the motorcycles have their sirens going, the women are rigid on their seats, their white helmets are spotless, they're on their way to Nice and all Charlie has to do there is buy the newspaper."

This time Eddy was sure he saw men between the trees, dressed in light-colored uniforms, different from the green tunics of the National Guardsmen.

"Did you notice something about Charlie's imagination?" Viola asked.

"Ostentatious lecherousness, hardly surprising when you know him, but good luck to him, I hope he pulls it off."

"I'm not in it."

"In what?"

"The Rolls. I'm never in his dreams, and he isn't in mine. *You* are in mine."

"That's nice," Eddy said. A jet plane coming in announced the proximity of the airport. They saw Las Mercedes's low buildings, grouped in a half circle around a control tower. The blue lights of the runways stretched like perfect radials far into the valley.

Viola squeezed Eddy's wrist again. "Another few days now. I heard that we can be in Germany within twenty-four hours."

Eddy parked the car and reached over Viola's thighs to open her door. "We won't see the Rembrandt until tomorrow evening and we may not be able to leave right away, there aren't too many flights and they're all booked up in advance."

Viola pulled the door shut again. "Let's not go yet, I haven't been so comfortable in a long time. I hope that the party won't be canceled again. The confusion here is fatiguing, all those nervous people who keep on changing their minds are getting to me. Charlie is so frantic he can hardly sit still, did he tell you where's he off to today?"

"Didn't Major Koboldski invite him for golf?"

"The Jerry with the scars on his cheeks?"

They got out of the car. Two urchins pushed each other aside, jabbering at Eddy.

"What do they want?"

Eddy jangled small change.

"Don't give them anything."

Eddy patted a boy on his narrow shoulder. "Here you are, amigo, do a good job." He smiled at Viola. "If you don't pay them they're likely to scratch the car or rip off the window wipers."

She squeezed her handbag under her arm. "So what, it isn't ours, is it? Off with you, get away."

The boys, dressed in man-sized, torn jackets and frayed jeans, stepped back and bowed, holding each other by the hand. Eddy bowed back. "They should be wearing straw hats and carrying canes. Good actors, don't you think?"

"I know their type, Italy is full of them. They'll steal the gold out of your teeth if they're given the chance."

The boys trotted off, their naked feet drawing lines in the dust of the parking lot.

Eddy walked to the main building; Viola ran after him. "Are you alone in the world? I'm on high heels, I can't walk that fast. Put your arm around me, I want to feel protected. Tell me we'll be rich soon."

"We'll be rich soon."

"Very rich?"

"Yes."

"How much?"

"A zillion gold pieces."

"Now tell me what you're planning to do with your zillion," Viola asked when they ordered drinks.

"Something quiet."

"With me, in our California palace?"

"In Amsterdam I thought."

She shook her head. "I don't want to go home, everything is petty there."

"Amsterdam isn't petty." He gave her the cherry out of his cocktail. She pressed the moist fruit between her lips, moved it around with her tongue and turned up her eyes.

Eddy suppressed a yawn. "Very sexy."

She swallowed too quickly and coughed. "You could put a little more enthusiasm in your voice. Are you jealous that I'm sleeping with Charlie every night?"

He watched a sleek American jet fighter being pulled away by a tractor. Heavily armed guardsmen surrounded the plane. Further along soldiers were running to a helicopter, the engine catching as soon as they jumped in. He saw them close the sliding door as the gigantic blade pulled the gray machine into the sky. Another chopper was offloading wounded men strapped to stretchers.

"Shall I tell you my cherry story?" Viola asked.

"Please."

"It's really my neighbor boy's tale, we were still little then, eight or nine years old. He always came to play with me and he would look up my bottom, it never seemed to occur to him that I was hollow on the other side too."

Eddy played with his glass. She paused significantly.

He forced himself to respond. "Yes?"

"He was a shy little boy who had created a magical world of his own. The woman who lived on the other side of the street was his princess, she must have been thirty years old and liked to walk around in transparent housecoats. Her husband worked in the zoo and once took a raccoon home, they kept the animal as a pet."

I'll have a cat in Amsterdam, Eddy thought, a fat cat, it can sleep on my lap when I read.

Viola took a carefully measured sip. "Okay, the bitch asked my friend if he wanted to meet the raccoon and he said he did, of course. She had her sex coat on again, the boy had to sit down at her feet and she sprawled on the couch. She asked the servant to bring her a drink and a lemonade for the kid. You know what the princess did then? Right in front of that innocent child?"

"No."

"She unbuttoned her peignoir and inserted the cherry that she had fished out of her drink between her legs and called the raccoon. The beast, who must have performed the trick many times before, trotted up obediently, took the cherry out, fiddled with it for a bit and then *ate* it."

Same shrill voice as that whore in Bogotá, Eddy thought, when she yelled at me after I walked away from her hut.

"What a performance that must have been. My friend came home in mental agony. Never recovered for as long as I knew him. Just imagine, his goddess turns out to be some cheap whore, and the poor child has to realize the truth on a beautiful summer morning. All his ideals squeezed to shit in a raccoon's hand, raccoons have real hands you know."

Eddy got up. "I'll be back in a moment."

He saw Viola's laughing mouth in the swirling circles of the toilet bowl; when he flushed again, he saw his own face, smiling at the victims of practical jokes in the villa at the Kleine Alster. He vomited and saw new scenes each time; clear pictures that followed each other in order, like framed prints in the neutral surroundings of a modern art gallery. Allied officers, including himself, heaved a grand piano out of a window and applauded when it splintered in the rock garden. Naked women squealed on a bar counter as they were sprayed with soda water. Onkel Franz was shot at with peas blown out of brass tubes. Scenes from jolly days long past but as detailed as Viola's fornicating raccoon. When his stomach was empty, he rinsed his mouth, washed his hands, and put on his jacket again.

"You look pale," she said when they drove back to Managua. "Was your stomach upset?"

"A little."

"I hope you don't have dysentery. Charlie brought the right drugs, I'll make him give you some tonight."

"I'm fine." He accelerated.

"I love it when you drive so fast."

There had been hardly any traffic, but when the car topped a crest the road was blocked. A truck filled with kneeling soldiers was stopped at an angle and another came from the opposite direction. There was no time to brake and Eddy turned the wheel. There wasn't enough shoulder left and he swerved further so that the Chrysler rode over a ditch, with two wheels up against a low earth wall. Boulders ahead made him force the wheel back again. The left front tire was back on the tarmac, making the car spin. It turned round completely and again hurled itself at the trucks. Eddy braked and aimed for the other side of the road. Viola cried out when the car bounced off a truck's fender.

"The tank is exploding," she yelled.

The explosions were rifle shots. Eddy restarted the stalled engine. Behind them the soldiers were firing into the jungle, pouring in bullets as fast as their automatic weapons allowed.

More trucks came lumbering up, followed by an armored car. Its cannon was shooting too, pumping high-explosive rounds into the dense mass of palms rising from thick undergrowth.

"Get away, Eddy, please, please."

He maneuvered between the trucks, hoping he wouldn't be hit, and pressed the gas pedal as soon as he saw an opening. More trucks were parked around the next curve, but he was driving slowly now and got past them unscathed. A jeep lay on its side; a corpse slumped over the spare tire. Again guardsmen were firing into the trees, obtaining no more results than leaves floating down and the trunks quivering briefly. A helicopter gunship hovering further along had its heavy weapons trained on the jungle's impassive mass and shook in the air as its tracer bullets zoomed between tree tops.

"They can shoot forever," Eddy said as they drove on, "and they won't even hit a bird."

"We could have been killed."

"We weren't."

"We *could* have been, and Charlie gets it all then."

"It's the risk of the game."

Viola's hands shook as she reached for his arm. "Oh, why didn't you kill Charlie in Empoli? It would have been easy then. It'll be easy here too, won't it? We can go for a drive or a walk and get rid of him on the way."

He pushed her hand away. "Stop that, Viola, there's plenty for all of us. You'll benefit more than we will anyway."

"How so?"

He shrugged. "You're young, we're old. Maybe we have ten years more, you have at least forty."

"I'll only get it all if you kill Charlie and then marry me."

"I won't do either."

They drove into a suburb; the Chrysler got lost in a web of winding streets, passing through a lane whose narrow sidewalks were crowded with women. The car's headlights illuminated spongy thighs and breasts, pushing through slit skirts and out of low blouses. Tinny music blared out of cafés, punctuated haphazardly by the horns of cars and mopeds.

"If you won't kill Charlie I will," Viola said. "I'll find a way. What do you mean, *either?*"

"I won't marry you," Eddy said loudly.

"In Amsterdam?" She laughed mockingly. "What will the neighbors say? You want me to live in sin with you?"

"I don't want you to live with me at all."

"What?"

"You heard me." Eddy had to brake suddenly to avoid a jaywalking prostitute. Viola banged her face against the windshield.

"Sorry, but that woman was in the way. Did you hurt yourself?"

"I want to get out of the car."

"Here?" Eddy asked. "I don't even know where we are."

She slipped out from under his restricting arm and pulled her handbag from between the seats. He tried again to stop her but she scratched his hand. Eddy wanted to get out of the car too, but a fat woman pressed her bosom against his chest. He looked into her toothless mouth.

"Complete number, gringo?"

He fell back onto the car seat while her hand, pretending to go for his crotch, slipped toward his pockets. He shoved her away and banged the door shut.

Eddy drove back to the hotel, leaving Viola stuck in the alley. The street women, thinking her to be foreign competition, ripped her blouse, hit her in the face, and kicked her shins as she tried to pass them. She yelled for help and a guardsman appeared, pulling her with him. He tried to push her into a portal once they were out of the street but gave up when she pointed her nails at his eyes. As she staggered through an avenue she broke the heel off her shoe and had to walk the last mile on stockinged feet.

Eddy was dozing in the lobby when she came in; she swung her purse against his knee as she walked by. He jumped up.

She limped to the elevator. The door started to close but Eddy blocked its electronic eye with his hand and went in after her. She was muttering and crying.

Eddy held her shoulders. "Charlie hasn't come back, I'll take you to your room. You'll feel better when you've had a shower." He poured a drink and took it to the bathroom. The glass rattled against her teeth. "You shouldn't have left me there."

"You didn't give me any choice. Couldn't you find a cab?"

"There weren't any."

The soles of her feet were black with grime, and he scrubbed them clean. She held on to him and stroked his hair. "Careful, darling, your suit is getting all wet."

"Come out, I'll dry you."

She stepped over the edge of the bath and dropped into his arms. "You still love me, don't you?"

He held on to her, soapy water dribbling down his trousers. Her clawing hands grabbed the lapels of his jacket. "Tell me you didn't mean what you said in the car."

"I did mean it."

She stepped back and stood in the middle of the room. Her hand pointed shakily at the door. "Get out."

He closed the door quietly behind him. From the corridor he heard falling furniture, breaking glass, and hysterical screaming.

"Tonight is the party," Viola said, "tomorrow we leave."

Eddy held up a carafe. "More coffee, anyone?"

A low rumble ebbed through the hotel's gardens and made its windows tinkle. "There goes another building," said Charlie. "The Guardia is blowing up an entire part of the city, Koboldski says that they haven't got enough men to risk hand-to-hand fighting." He wiped his mouth with a napkin. "I like machines, don't you? Why bother with heroics if you can flatten the enemy location with a few well-placed bombs and then burn what comes out with napalm?"

"I don't know," Viola said, "if you kill everybody you run short of servants in the end. Do you want coffee or don't you, Eddy is waiting."

"Please."

Eddy poured. They were the only guests in the breakfast room; a waiter in a white suit set off with gold braid was polishing glasses behind the buffet, another contemplated his immaculate shoes. The view was quiet too, freshly mown lawns giving way to fancy shrubbery adorned with brightly colored flowers.

Bang.

Charlie jumped up. "A rifle shot, and close too."

"A hunter." Eddy looked at the waiters. One held up a shiny

glass before putting it away on a shelf, the other yawned behind his hand. "We're next door to the palace and the Guardia is all around us, I think we're safe here. Where's the party tonight?"

Charlie had his nose pressed against the window. "Sit down," Viola said, "and answer. Eddy asked you a question."

Charlie came back reluctantly. "At the president's mansion at the Laguna Ticapa. Koboldski is fetching us by car this afternoon."

"Far away?"

"About an hour from Las Mercedes by helicopter."

"And the Rembrandt is in the mansion?"

Charlie forgot his fear. "Hoho. Of course. Koboldski finally presented me to the president last night and I set him up nicely. Got him in his weak spot all right. Maybe he's a genius and a power symbol, but he's as vain as the next man, all it needed was a little flattery. Tickled pink that art historians from Europe are here to admire his Rembrandt."

Viola tweaked his cheek. "Good, we're proud of you. So tonight we photograph the map."

"Don't do that." Charlie rubbed his face. "I've just shaved, you know how sensitive my skin is."

"Who takes the photograph?" Eddy asked.

"I will. I'll say that there isn't enough light in the room and ask permission to take the painting off the wall. You take it from me and fumble about, making quite sure its back side is visible. Meanwhile Viola can distract his attention."

"Sounds fine," Viola said. "I'm going upstairs, I slept badly and tonight is the night."

Bang.

"There he is" — Eddy pointed at the window — "a butterfly hunter."

"A what?" Charlie asked.

"Haven't you seen the giant butterflies here? I suppose he shoots them and then sells them to collectors."

"What a beautiful man," Viola said. "I like these Indian males, they're so graceful, but very masculine too."

Charlie threw down his napkin. "Crazy. Nobody shoots butterflies. The fellow hunts songbirds, I've seen them in the stores, you can buy them by the dozen, a delicacy."

"Butterflies," Eddy said stubbornly. "I think I'll lie down too. What time is Koboldski coming?"

"At two."

Bang. A small dainty body fluttered down above the shrubs.

Viola stared at the hunter. "Isn't he handsome? I would love to have him as a butler. He wouldn't be expected to do much, just dress up in some lovely uniform with a red sash."

"He would have to do plenty," Charlie said and stalked out of the room. The waiter caught the door as it swung back and bowed to Viola.

"Are you coming?" Viola asked, but Eddy was still gazing out of the window and didn't seem to hear her.

*

Charlie lay on his bed, his mouth half-open as he snored softly. His eyes moved restlessly beneath their closed lids. He was walking on the lawn behind the hotel and followed the hunter. Charlie walked somewhat stooped, swinging his arms in an exaggerated fashion as if he wanted to express suitable servility. The hunter moved with long dancing steps and Charlie had to run to keep up. Then the hunter spread his arms and floated up. Charlie jumped and flapped his arms, but the earth sucked his dense body back; he fell and scrambled up again. Large, bright orange birds glided ahead of the hunter and were hit by his soundless bullets. The birds planed gently before they dropped on the hunter's outstretched hand. He rolled them up and inserted them into tubes attached to leather bandoliers strapped across his wide naked chest. As soon as the birds were put away, they changed into gold bars, protruding from the tubes, reflecting sunlight on both ends.

Charlie was too tired to drag himself up from the ground and crawled forward on his knees. The hunter had filled his bandoliers and looked at his kneeling shadow.

"Yes?"

Charlie's meekness grew. Why did the hunter want him to formulate his request, didn't he know Charlie's desire?

"Yes?" the hunter asked again.

Charlie stuttered. "M . . . may I have the gold?"

Points of cold light glittered in the hunter's eyes, emitting sharp rays that raked across Charlie's skull, causing much pain.

"Why should I give you the gold?" The hunter's voice rumbled, making every nerve in Charlie's body vibrate.

"Because I serve you," Charlie whispered.

This was the truth, he should not be required to clarify his statement. If the hunter did not grasp Charlie's meaning, this meeting could not be true, even if he were dreaming. I know I'm dreaming, Charlie thought, but the dream is true. He felt the stubbles of the newly cut grass prick into his knees, heard the sharp leaves of palm trees rub against each other. He was also aware of the hunter's penetrating power, which forced him to be what he was, now, in the past, and forever. He had always been the hunter's servant, and servants have to be paid from time to time.

The hunter smiled and the pain in Charlie's head increased. "Very well." The gold bars loosened themselves from the hunter's bandoliers and fluttered toward Charlie, again becoming birds.

"Thank you." Charlie bowed until his forehead touched the grass. The birds covered his body when he pushed himself up. He hopped over the lawn, carried by the birds' wings dusted with gold.

For a moment the pain became part of his ecstasy. Possession hurts marvelously, Charlie thought. But how long could he bear the sharp beaks that cut through his skin? He yelled in agony when he saw that the birds were stripping the skin from his bones, eating their way into his flesh, digging tunnels toward his heart and stomach, yanking muscles and nerves away from the bones.

Maybe this is an orgasm of joy, Charlie thought, it will stop in a moment, I will be allowed to rest.

The pain got worse.

"Take them back," shouted Charlie.

"I cannot," the hunter said, "they are yours."

"Take them back."

"Don't squawk like that," Viola said, "and stop kicking me. I'm trying to sleep too."

Charlie sat up.

"Were you dreaming?" Viola asked.

"Yes, about birds." He wanted to tell her the dream but she turned over and he couldn't remember much of it anyway. "And the hunter."

"Do shut up," Viola said.

*

Viola tried to understand how the weapon worked. It was the hunter's rifle; she studied its worn barrel and slightly cracked wooden butt. Her finger circled the trigger.

I'm dreaming, she thought, and in a dream anything goes. If I want to shoot, I shoot. She waved the rifle and ran along an immense lawn that stretched beyond the horizon. Where were the birds? They had to be around somewhere. In answer a flock rose from the flowering shrubs.

She stopped and took aim. The birds were golden with long tails and wings and tufted heads. She fired and saw her shots strike home. The birds fell out of the sky and splashed the lawn with their colors, lying quite still, like small fans forgotten after a Japanese tea party. She swept them together and carried them in her skirt. She skipped around the lawn laughing until a foul smell wafting up made her look down. The birds' heads were twisted and broken and their ruffled feathers covered with putrid slime. She let go of her skirt; the corpses fell and formed a rotting heap.

This is impossible, Viola thought. They are my golden birds.

The hunter stood close. She saw the muscles on his chest swell and his moist skin shine. His long black hair writhed as if he were dancing, but his body was still.

"These birds are no good," Viola said.

203

The hunter knelt down and stroked the lifeless little bodies. The birds trembled; their small heads came alive, their tails taut. They flew up and settled on the hunter's arms, changing him into a winged god.

"Aren't they mine?" Viola asked.

The hunter rose slowly.

"I want to have you too," Viola said. "You hold what I need. I adore you."

The hunter spread his vast and gorgeous wings. I'm dreaming, Viola thought, and the dream is getting away from me. She picked up the rifle. Its barrel drooped down and she rubbed it to make it stiff again. The rifle faded away and she was looking at her empty hands, then her hands became transparent too.

"Stay with me!" Viola heard herself shriek.

The hunter began to float into the air. She jumped forward and tried to grab hold of his slender feet. "What am I without you?" She had to look away, for his eyes were filled with clear intense light. "I will serve you faithfully."

"You cannot," the hunter said. His deep voice filled her with desire for a moment. Her hooked nails slid off his feet. His feathers shone. His wings beat once and he soared into the sky. The sun burned the lawn. White flames leaped up at her.

She saw Charlie lying next to her, reading the paper.

"Close the blinds," Viola said, "the light is hurting my eyes."

"Close them yourself," Charlie said.

*

Eddy tried to hold on to the book that was sliding out of his hand, but the hunter already faced him. I'm dreaming, Eddy thought, and this dream will be too much for me, I have to wake up at once. The hunter laughed.

"What's so funny?" Eddy asked.

"You." Eddy recognized the hunter but he also looked like Kroll and Lerche; that part of the resemblance had to be absurd, an Indian god is no fat German, and no thin German either.

"I thought you up myself," Eddy said, "and I must be losing control. Get away from me."

"This is no time for nonsense," the hunter said, "I come to bring you what you have always sought."

Eddy staggered back. An immense butterfly with pale red wings perched on the hunter's outstretched arm; its color changed to gold as it edged closer. It grew as it approached and its eyes were made of ice.

"What good is it to me?"

"You helped to shape it," the hunter said, "and it has come to be accepted."

"I have no need of it."

"It will provide anything you can imagine, it is my gift to you, and the gift of the others."

"You have been dead for almost thirty years," Eddy said, "I saw you being dragged from the school's moat. The truck got Kroll, and Lerche is picking green beans in Three Oak."

"We are all here, right now, joined in the butterfly."

The hunter and the butterfly merged into one shape, stronger and fiercer than its originals. The hunter's supple power was in the insect, and the insect's obsessive desire was in the hunter.

"You have to take me," they said together, "because we are the result of your own deeds. You evoked us and we are here to serve you or destroy you. Don't you know what we can mean to you?"

"The villa in California, a hellish paradise?"

"Or the house in Amsterdam. You want to study, don't you? We will make you grasp anything at once; no matter how you use us, the result will always be profitable."

"I can refuse," Eddy said.

The creature hissed at him. "How can you refuse? Do you think that you can choose now when you have never chosen before?"

"I chose to live."

"Not willingly."

"And now I choose to die."

"Then you will have to fight us."

Eddy attacked but the battle was unequal. The enemy could fly and swept down from odd angles. Eddy lost at every contact; he could hear his bones shatter as his eyes were blinded by blood.

There'll be nothing left of me, Eddy thought, but he fought on although he couldn't get hold of the being's smooth golden wings. Its cruelly curved spurs and sharp claws cut through his flesh.

I gave up the treasure, Eddy thought, I don't need a victory either.

A wing hooked into his hand and his fingers closed over it. Dry segments snapped off at his touch. The enemy stumbled about him. Eddy could see again and tried to caress its head. The head broke off beneath his hand.

The hunter emerged out of the crumbling corpse and smiled.

"You always said yes, how do you feel now that you've said no?"

"Let me embrace you," Eddy said.

His head rested on the hunter's sweaty shoulder; the hunter's strong hand stroked Eddy's back.

Somebody knocked on the door. Eddy got up and unlocked it.

"You're wet all over," Viola said.

"I was dreaming about my brother."

"I didn't know you had a brother."

"He died when I was a kid."

"You should get dressed," Viola said, "the palace car will be here soon."

"This is our most beautiful season," the president said, "and it's much nicer outside than inside. That's why I had dinner served on the terrace. Please follow me."

The mansion was built on a cape, with a perfect view of the lagoon. A veiled moon softened the mountains' contours on the far side of the water and illuminated smooth waves speckled with floating seagulls. Crickets sang in the bushes surrounding a rock garden; goldfish flickered in a pond at the terrace's side. Two motionless guardsmen, rifles ready, stood on the bridge connecting the terrace with the garden.

"We are quite safe here," a portly general said and offered his arm to Viola. "Allow me to escort you to your chair." He pointed at the fine meshed netting connecting the roof's rafters with the low wall dividing terrace and garden. "The screens will defend us against the mosquitos and the soldiers against the guerrillas. The guerrillas are the lesser of two evils, we know how to deal with them, but mosquitos are too small to shoot."

Viola looked at the bay. "How beautifully silent it is here, and what a lovely garden the president has."

The general nodded approvingly. "Indeed, señora, an exceptional location." He addressed himself to the president. "If God would live on earth he would certainly choose a similar site ... if he could afford it."

Everybody laughed. Major Koboldski's elbow dug into Eddy's side. "Old buffoon, likes to repeat his jokes but the president is always amused." Koboldski had spoken in German; the general held up a correcting finger. "We only speak *Christiano* at this table, major."

His audience laughed again, the president roared and lifted his glass. "You're doing very well tonight, general." He turned to Charlie. "And, Señor Vrieslander, was your work satisfactory? I hope we didn't get in your way too much."

Charlie's knuckle hit the camera that he had put down on the table. "Not at all, Señor Presidente. There are some excellent photographs in this thing now. We are very grateful indeed. The queen has personally asked me to do everything possible to include the *Absalom* in the book she is paying for, and we would not have been able to grant her wish without your cooperation. Our queen is very fond of biblical subjects."

The host's knife swished through a juicy steak, fresh red slices fell against each other; the president looked up from his occupation. "One head of state should help another. Do you know that my colleague in Guatemala also owns a Rembrandt?"

"Really?" Charlie asked, blending a tone of proper excitement and respect into his voice.

"You didn't know? I can telephone him if you like and you will be able to photograph his painting too."

"Yes?"

"Now isn't that a special treat? Two birds with one stone?"

"Two butterflies," Viola said. "Yes, darling, why don't you go to Guatemala too?"

"Another biblical subject?" Eddy asked. The president's gaze attached itself to Viola's almost completely exposed breasts, and Eddy had to repeat his question.

"Pardon? No." Laugh wrinkles pressed together around the president's bloodshot eyes. "But I won't mind telling you what the painting represents, provided that the ladies will excuse me beforehand." He looked at his female guests one by one, leaving Viola for last. "Yes? You don't mind, Señora Vrieslander?"

"I am a modern woman."

"Very well then," the president said. "If a master painter from the glorious past allows himself to portray a certain scene, a simple state official should be permitted to describe the happening in words. Well, the painting represents a young lady. She is, how shall I say it?" His gaze feasted on Viola's bosom again. "... rather well formed and hasn't dressed yet. She is lying down on a four-poster bed and seems to be, eh, bored. She doesn't have anything particular to do, I suppose that's what it was."

The general was grinning in anticipation but coughed apologetically when the president's forbidding hand flicked in his direction. The president looked at Eddy. "And the lady — she is young and energetic, isn't she? — wants to have something to do."

"Certainly," Eddy said politely.

"So she amuses herself, with a cushion."

"With a cushion?" Charlie asked.

"Yes, you may guess what she's doing with the cushion."

"She embraces it?"

"More intimate, Señor Vrieslander."

Charlie shook his head.

"I will help you along a little. It is a large square seventeenth-century cushion, a *decorated* seventeenth-century cushion."

Charlie grinned eagerly. "Aha. With tassels. A tassel on each corner?"

The president tried not to laugh, his self-control made the leather of his Sam Browne–style belt creak. "She embraces the cushion, you're right in that respect, and she is an athletic young lady, she has raised her legs. The cushion is square, so how many tassels do you think the painting shows?"

"Three!" cheered Charlie.

The gentlemen guffawed; the local ladies hid their smiling mouths behind their fans. Viola laughed too. "Ho ho ho," bellowed the general, "capital joke! Three tassels! Ho ho ho!"

"Well, Señor Vrieslander, do you still want to go to Guatemala?"

"No," said Charlie, "I don't think that the queen . . ."

"I didn't think so either." The president clapped his hands. A servant came running to his side. "Ice cream for me, Alphonso, but I venture that the guests would like something a little more exotic. Tell me what the kitchen supplies today for dessert."

The waiter bowed. "Certainly, Señor Presidente. We have chocolate mousse, crêpes flambées . . ."

"Yes," Viola said, "a nice crêpe."

The guests agreed with her choice and Alphonso pushed in a cart on which all the paraphernalia necessary to prepare the delicacy were exhibited. While he mixed his special sauce, Viola told an anecdote relating how her father had taken her to an expensive restaurant that prided itself on its haute cuisine. Some of its more subtle dishes were traditionally prepared next to the guests' table. Her father, a finicky man who disliked the smell of cooking, objected. " 'Don't you have a kitchen in this joint?' The cook was furious," Viola said. "I blushed for days after that."

The general took a deep breath but wasn't given the opportunity to launch a fresh "ho ho." The first volley hit him in the chest, and blood spouting from between his medals splashed on the naked shoulder of his companion, who was suddenly leaning against him. She had been hit in the throat, and the impact of the bullets made her head snap back so that her glazed eyes stared at the ceiling. The shots came from the garden; one of the guardsmen had also been hit and hung in the mosquito screens that tore away slowly under his weight. Guardias came running from the house to assist the remaining soldier in the garden; their automatic arms rattled through the volleys that were still coming in.

The president dropped sideways, chair and all; Major Koboldski followed his example, pulling Eddy with him. Eddy grabbed Viola's ankles and dragged her under the table. He made sure that she wasn't hurt before he ordered her to crawl into the house.

She sobbed in fear. "And what if they're in there too?"

"They aren't, the shooting comes from the garden."

"Come with me, Eddy."

"In a minute."

He crawled to the guardsman lying on the terrace and picked up the man's weapon. Khaki-clad shapes fought outside with the soldiers who had emerged from the house, and Eddy saw the flash of bayonets and knives. One guerrilla was running away through the bushes, his head low to avoid bullets coming from the terrace. Eddy pressed his rifle's trigger without result; the fallen guardsman had already emptied its magazine. He felt through the corpse's pockets and found a spare clip, detached the empty one, and clicked its replacement into position. The guerrilla had turned around and charged the terrace. Eddy touched the trigger briefly to prevent emptying the magazine immediately. The three or four bullets released by the weapon connected with the man's face and chest with such force that he tottered and flopped over backward. The grenade he was about to throw fell and rolled toward Eddy, and he kicked it into the pond. It exploded as he dived back to the balcony's tiled floor, water cascading over him. A goldfish slithered near his head, gasping for air and twisting its tail fin.

Eddy struggled to his feet and saw Alphonso collapse slowly, the cognac bottle still in his hand. The servant's shiny white tunic was embellished with a star-shaped bloodstain in the exact location of his heart. Officers hiding behind overturned furniture emptied their revolvers while wiping food off their uniforms; the ladies had fled via the steps at the side of the terrace. The last one, a young woman in a sky-blue evening gown, writhed on the landing, holding her exposed intestines with both hands. She kept her mouth tightly closed as if it were unbecoming to groan in the presence of gentlemen. At the table the dead general and his silent companion rested peacefully in each other's arms. Eddy crawled to the threshold, carrying the guardsman's short rifle in his lower arms. Its bayonet got stuck in the carpet when he slid into the room; he yanked it free as he faced the porch. The corpses in the garden sprawled in the grass like tropical cats sucking up cool air from the soil. The enemy was invisible, and apparently reinforced — its steady fire now coming from several positions simultaneously.

"Eddy?" Viola lay next to him. "Where is the camera?"

"Charlie must have it, but I don't know what happened to him."

"It's probably still on the table outside," Viola said. "Will you get it?"

He crawled back. The camera strap dangled from the tabletop. Eddy yanked it; the camera dropped into his hand while sweeping bullets splintered glasses and bottles. A helicopter engine started up behind the building as he passed the threshold again.

Viola pointed. "All the officers escaped through that door. I saw Koboldski too, he was dragging Charlie with him, I think Charlie had fainted."

The machine's chopping sounded above the house. "There they go," Eddy said. "So what are we doing here?" Bullets whined through the room and loosened plaster rained down on them. Viola pressed herself against a large stone planter that had been cemented to the wall. The Rembrandt hung above the planter. Absalom stared thoughtfully at Eddy from his throne. A window shattered and a hand grenade hit the floor and bounced across the carpet.

"Into the planter!" shouted Eddy. Viola looked at him stupidly. He lifted her up and dropped her into the earth, pushed her to the side and lay down next to her; their bodies crushed leaves and flowers and squashed them into the moist soil. Viola tried to free herself from his embrace. He pressed her face down but she jerked her head free again, spitting earth at him.

He pulled her closer to him. "Be quiet."

The grenade still hadn't exploded. Eddy looked over the planter's concrete side and saw a guerrilla entering the room. The man walked on as the grenade burst; he yelled and staggered back, hit by several fragments. Burning metal hit the Rembrandt and tore it off the wall, flames licking across its surface as it fell on the carpet.

Eddy jumped out of the planter and picked up his rifle, dragging Viola out of the planter at the same time. She struggled to get loose. "Where can we go?"

"Outside."

"That's where the guerrillas are."

Eddy emptied his gun in the direction of the terrace to cover their retreat. "They're here too. We'll have more space outside."

The door led to a corridor connecting the front rooms with an inner court. Viola ran around like a trapped mouse. Eddy caught her and pushed her into a jeep parked next to crates packed with imported liquors and canned food. The engine started promptly, but he released the clutch too quickly and the jeep jumped briefly before stalling. He started it again. The doors of the courtyard gate weren't closed and he pushed them open with the jeep's bumper.

"Eddy. Hey!"

"That's Charlie," yelled Viola, "keep going."

Eddy reversed. Charlie grabbed hold of the spare tire; Eddy bent back and pulled him into the jeep. Charlie tumbled in sideways. "They left me behind, the camera is still on the dining table. We need it, if we can't get to it maybe we can grab the Rembrandt. We have to go back."

"I have the camera," shouted Eddy, "the painting is destroyed. Hold on."

The jeep roared through the gate and into two guerrillas who came running toward them. Eddy drove on; the jeep bounced over them. He shifted into second gear and stamped on the gas pedal. Another group of guerrillas appeared, busy mounting a machine gun on a tripod. The soldiers jumped out of the speeding jeep's path.

Charlie shouted into Eddy's ear. "There will be more of them ahead, try to get off the road."

The jeep's body almost tore off its chassis as the vehicle suddenly changed direction. It skipped on, along an uneven path through the jungle.

The track narrowed, illuminated by the jeep's leaping lights. The car's windshield was down and Viola had lowered herself between the seat and the dashboard. Charlie groaned in the rear.

Eddy braked when a thornbush scratched his skull. The jeep

was almost stopped when its left front wheel hit a large boulder. As the jeep leaped up on one side, a twisted limb hooked around Eddy's head, lifting him from his seat. The jeep stalled in the bushes a few yards further along.

Eddy hung, too surprised to move. The branch seemed to increase its pressure.

I'm not hanging by my hair, Eddy thought, because I haven't got any hair. I'm hanging by my neck. My neck isn't broken. The biblical situation was quite different. Absalom couldn't pull himself up and free his head. I can.

Charlie took the rifle from between the jeep's front seats, jumped down, and tottered toward Eddy.

He wants to kill me, Eddy thought and grabbed hold of the branch with both hands, forcing his head back, so that the forked wood no longer squeezed his neck.

I'm hanging loose, Eddy thought. I can drop down. Charlie doesn't know that, and he is unaware that I emptied the gun in the house. All he can do is try to stab me, but I know how I can block his attack. I will kill him in self-defense and obtain the gold so that I've won once and for all.

So that you have lost once and for all, the butterfly hunter said.

I have no other choice, Eddy thought.

If that were true there would be no other possibility, and you will again not have chosen.

Eddy saw the other possibility and smiled.

Charlie stabbed three times.

Viola stood between the oak and the jeep. Eddy's body fell at Charlie's feet. Viola's voice was so hoarse that Charlie couldn't make out what she said. "What?" Charlie asked. Charlie's voice wasn't clear either.

"The camera is in the side pocket of his jacket," Viola said. "Take it, so we can leave."

"Bah," Charlie said and tried to wipe his hands clean with his handkerchief.

"That isn't blood," Viola said, "that's the reflection of the jeep's taillights."

"**F**uck off," Charlie said to the two urchins who obstructed his way. "I carry my gear myself. I won't give you anything."

Charlie carried a suitcase and a satchel; Viola had already reached the airport's main building and was talking to Major Koboldski and a lieutenant.

Charlie's camera swung around him by its strap while he tried to free himself from the boys who were pulling at his baggage. He hit the naked legs of the more daring of the two with a vigorous blow of his suitcase. The impact made the boy stumble and fall, and the other ran away. Charlie walked on and greeted the major. Koboldski touched his cap. "Ah, Herr Vrieslander, I came to say good-bye."

"Now isn't that sweet of the major?" asked Viola. "He came personally to make sure that we have seats. It seems that this is the last scheduled flight out of Managua."

"For the time being," Koboldski said. "The countryside is at peace, but the fighting is now centered around the capital and the companies do not want to risk their valuable airplanes. Within a few days order will be restored, but I can imagine that you do not want to wait that long. May I offer you a farewell drink? You still have an hour to go. The lieutenant will take care that your luggage is taken aboard, and if you give him your tickets he will obtain your boarding passes."

Major Koboldski chewed the olive that he had taken from his empty martini glass. "The president asked me to convey his sincere apologies to you and regrets the confusion during the dinner and the resulting loss of Herr Sachs."

"Thank you," Charlie said.

The major spread his hands. "You understand that it was my first duty to make sure that the head of state was safe, but you have also seen how quickly we returned. Every guerrilla who took part in the attack has been killed, we managed to shoot most of them from the helicopters and the few who escaped were caught later and executed on the spot. It is unfortunately impossible to be sufficiently aware of surprise attacks, but we always win in the end."

"I'm sure you do," Charlie said, "and I sympathize with the problematical situation here, but I will tell you that I was pleased when I saw your helicopter pop up."

Koboldski smoothed a crease in his tunic. "And I was glad to see you. It was good that you had found that open spot; if you had stayed in the jungle we would have been searching for quite a while."

"Did you manage to find Eddy?" Viola asked.

"Yes, Frau Vrieslander, with some trouble. The track through the forest is not too visible from the sky, but one of our pilots saw vultures circling above the jungle and alerted a ground patrol by radio."

Viola shivered.

"By the way," Koboldski said, "it isn't too clear to me how Herr Sachs came to his end. You said that you met some guerrillas on the path?"

Viola looked at Charlie.

"Four men," said Charlie. "They tried to stop us but I drove on. The jeep was bouncing over boulders and Eddy fell out. The guerrillas were shooting at us and because I wasn't armed I could only keep on driving."

Koboldski's hand rubbed his perfectly shaven jowls. *"Ach so?*

But we have been able to trace the attack route of the guerrillas. They arrived on small boats following the lagoon's coastline and approached the mansion through the front garden. After that a group split away from the main body and attacked the house from the side. The forest track was not on their itinerary."

"They were there," Charlie said, "Eddy's corpse is the proof."

"And then there is the riddle of the weapon that was used and that we found next to the body," Koboldski said. "Herr Sachs was stabbed with a bayonet attached to an M-16, only our Guardia Nacional uses American weapons. The guerrillas are armed with Russian-made submachine guns."

Charlie shrugged. "Perhaps they stole the weapon from the National Guard."

"Could be," Koboldski said. "Yes?"

The lieutenant bent down and whispered into Koboldski's ear. The major jumped up. "I'm afraid that there are some complications. We are under attack. Your airplane is now ready to leave."

The lieutenant whispered again.

"Unfortunately there is only one seat available. You will have to excuse me. Duty calls."

Charlie watched speechlessly as Koboldski clicked his heels and ran off. The lieutenant placed a boarding pass on the table and trotted after his superior.

Viola reached for the piece of green cardboard but Charlie grabbed her hand. "That's what you would like, right? This time it's my turn." Viola got up. Charlie knocked her back into her chair.

Viola reached the hall where groups of panic-stricken passengers milled about. Guardsmen contained the shouting and pushing mass and slowly withdrew to the fence where passengers with boarding passes were allowed through.

"Charlie!"

Charlie heard her but didn't look around. He had forced himself through the exit and joined the passengers who were stumbling toward the waiting plane.

The two boys, curious and excited by the chaos, had run around the building and reached the runway where they watched the airline company's employees guiding the passengers to the plane. One boy jumped up and down and pointed at Charlie. *"Hijo maldito de puta podrida."*

"True," the other boy said, "but let's not be idle. Let's steal something."

They worked their way through the passengers, flicking their pocketknives open, moving stealthily.

Charlie sat in the airplane, taxiing away. The dull explosions of mortar shells thudded steadily, audible even through the din of the jet's engines. Clouds of dust and rubble appeared on the runway ahead. The plane roared, missed the holes, and took off at full power. The passengers applauded as its wheels retracted. Charlie sat back and laughed.

"I have the map." Charlie sniggered. His hands felt for the camera's reassuring presence, but it didn't seem to be there. He released the safety belt and got up, still smiling. It would have slipped to the side, the camera that contained the map to the gold. He saw the strap and yanked it out from between the seats and stood feeling both ends, cut cleanly, holding nothing.